They Don't Play Stickball in Milwaukee

by

Reed Farrel Coleman

THE PERMANENT PRESS
SAG HARBOR, NY 11963

Coleman, Reed Farrel.
  They Don't Play Stickball in Milwaukee/by Reed Farrel Coleman
      p.   cm.
  ISBN 1-877946-95-8
  I. Title.
  PS3553.047445T48
  813'.54--dc20   96-46356
                                                      CIP

First edition, December 1997

THE PERMANENT PRESS
4170 Noyac Road
Sag Harbor, NY 11963

Dedicated to the memory of my late parents,
Bea and Herb Coleman

Prologue

Angel

Angel Hernandez's skin was an elaborate puzzle of fire-breathing tattoos and Christ heads. Some of the body art was delicate, subtle like the flecks of bright red in the tar-black eyes of the dragon which stretched its scaly wings across Angel's back. The ominous talons, raised at anyone who noticed the dragon—it was impossible not to notice—held a crucifix. The dying Christ seemed unfazed. The jagged tail ran the length of Angel's spine, spiraling around a black dagger on his right buttock. The white face of Christ superimposed on a red cross covered his hairless chest. This was a skilled piece of work as well. The tattoos of blue chains around his neck and upper arms were sloppy, but had a certain flair.

There were others, amateurish gang markings that let the rest of the prison population know under whose protection Angel traveled. He had carved *Madre* into his right forearm over and over again until a blind man could read the raised scar tissue. He had carved another word, a name, into the skin of his upper left thigh near the crease between his leg and groin. The letters in the name were ragged and undetectable even to other men in the shower. Only the weaker prisoners Angel preyed upon and sodomized knew the name was there at all. He often beat his prey for asking about the name. After the first few years, only the uniniti-ated wondered aloud.

Christ and the painted dragon cried tears of Angel's sweat as he strained to finish his third set of ten reps bench-ing three hundred pounds. He was already souless and a murderer when he got to Attica, but rage and time had con-spired with free weights to turn the rest of him into stone.

"Come on, Angel, two more," the spotter yelled at Hernandez.

"*Nueve*," Angel grunted, pushing the bar up and locking his elbows. "Did you get it out for me?"

"Come on, one more, we talk when you're done."

"Did you get the fucking thing out for me?" Angel

screamed at his spotter, his arms beginning to shake from the strain.

"Yeah, man. Okay, okay. I got it out. I got it out."

Angel let the bar drop slowly to his chest and he pushed it back up to complete his reps. He placed the bar in the Y-shaped rests on either side of the bench and sat up. He walked to where his shirt covered a pack of cigarettes. He flipped the pack to his spotter. Smiling broadly, the spotter shook the pack close by his ear.

"Don't worry, *pato*," Angel assured him, "there's enough Dilaudid in dat pack to keep you and your beetch happy for de month."

*   *   *

At mess that night, three guards surrounded Angel when he went to clear his tray. They herded him into a storage room off the kitchen. He was handcuffed, his legs shackled, and a sock was stuffed in his mouth. Angel didn't resist, there was too much at stake.

"We hear you're leavin' us next week for the halfway house. And me and some of the boys were kinda hurt you didn't tell us. But we're not the type a people to hold a grudge, no sir. So we thought we'd throw ya this little bye-bye party."

Angel tensed his muscles, waiting for the first fist or baton blow to crack his ribs. No blows came. Instead the guards just laughed at Angel. The guard who had done the talking motioned his two partners away from the prisoner. He stepped back from Angel and pulled out a Taser. He let Angel get a good look at the electro-shock gun. Now Angel tried to run, but even before he could trip over his shackled ankles, the tethered hook caught his shirt. His bones burned in pain as his skin crawled with a million unseen ants. His body convulsed wildly and he could smell his own filth as his muscles lost all control. He didn't remember passing out.

He woke up with a start, unchained and in his cell. He'd been cleaned up, but he was sick to his stomach, his head on the edge of explosion. Angel staggered out of his bunk,

8

straining to see the calendar in the dark. The dates hadn't changed, just seven days more. He felt the wall for his brother's picture. He kissed the snapshot, crossed himself, climbed back into his bunk. He slide his right hand under the waistband of his pants and felt for the name carved into his thigh. Angrily whispering the inscribed name, Angel cried himself to sleep.

County Jail

County jail was not prison. It wasn't her mother's warm embrace, but it wasn't prison. Prison was coming. She no longer viewed her trial with any remote sense of optimism. When she found herself entertaining even vaguely hopeful thoughts, she bit the inside of her lip until blood gushed across her tongue. The taste of blood reminded her not to hope. She saw her trial only as a rest stop on the way to prison, a bureaucratic hiccup, a way for the masses to avoid culpability. Never mind that she was innocent, she was going away for the better part of twenty years.

"Prison." She liked to say the word. She liked to play with the word. "On. Sip. Son. No. Sin. In. Nip. Pin. Sir."

But it wouldn't be called a prison, not where she was headed. It would be called a correctional facility for women. She wondered what flaws in her character the facility would be correcting. She wondered what she would do with her days and how long it would be before she was raped by a guard or one of the other correctees.

Women had come on to her in county, but she'd been able to turn down the offers without much trouble. The state had a vested interest in keeping her protected at least until the charade of the trial was through. But she had decided to surrender to the next woman who approached her. Better to face it and get it over with, she thought. Maybe she could learn to like it. The dream was all tapped out of her, leaving numbness in its stead.

She wouldn't be old when she got out, but that was somehow moot. She already felt old, ancient, tired. She just wanted to go to sleep and sleep until she turned to dust. Unfortunately the mechanisms which protected her from the other women in county also protected her from her dreams of sleep. In one sense, she couldn't wait for the trial to be done with. She had even toyed with the idea of copping a plea. And then, in the dark of her cell, she could lay herself down to sleep.

Mississippi

Johnny MacClough had just finished pulling the stool down off the bar top when the Scupper's front door opened. Marty Camp, dusting snow off his blue tunic, dropped a bound pile of mail on the bar.

"Anything for me?" Marty asked.

"Nothing," MacClough answered, already skimming the bundle.

"Anything from Dylan?"

"Yeah, a postcard from the La Brea Tar Pits: 'MacClough, These dumb dinosaurs had a better chance in the tar pits than I do of selling my mss. Miss the Scupper. Miss Sound Hill. Mississippi. See you soon. Klein.'"

"The eternal optimist," Camp remarked. "How long's he been out on the left coast?"

"Five whole days."

Camp shook his head and went back out into the snow. MacClough poured himself a cup of coffee and finished weeding through the mail. Mostly, it was the usual tripe: bills, more bills, and solicitations. Everybody had something to sell you and unconvincing reasons why you just had to buy it. MacClough ripped up the direct mailings, though he would have much preferred to shred the bills. Late January wasn't the high season for pubs on the east end of Long Island.

There was one letter in the bunch. It had no return address on the envelope. MacClough shook the envelope like a pack of sugar and tore off one edge. He took out the one sheet of paper and read it three or four times. He went behind the bar and picked up a bottle of Murphy's Irish Whiskey. He noticed the bottle was shaking in his hand. Unsuccessfully, he tried willing his hand steady.

He poured a few drops into his coffee before abandoning that idea. Instead, he removed the pouring spout and pressed his lips around the bottle mouth. MacClough tilted his head back and the bottle up. With a quarter bottle in him, he stopped to look at his hand. The shaking hadn't stopped, but he no longer cared. The Irish had done its job.

11

Pillow

Harry Klein had all the time in the world to sleep, he just never could. If it wasn't the pain that kept him up, it was the anticipation. He sat back in bed against a stack of pillows, the room black but for the glow of the television. His eyes were aimed in the direction of the glow, but he wasn't watching. Harry's right thumb pressed the channel button every two seconds. Something flashed onto the screen, something flashed off the screen. He could feel the first hints of pain in his left hip. After a lifetime of pain, Harry had gotten good at recognizing the initial onset. It was sort of like knowing you're going to sneeze, except what Harry was feeling bore no resemblance to that tickley feeling in your nose.

He started to sweat, feeling to see if his pain patch was in place. It was. At times, he could swear the druggist had gotten it wrong and given him nicotine patches. Switching the remote to his left hand, he reached across his body fumbling for his pills. Remarkably, he opened the bottle with one hand and popped a capsule in his mouth. Swallowing was reflexive. Harry had gotten past the need for water decades ago. During this whole time, his left thumb continued clicking through the channels.

Harry braced himself. He knew the hints would become twinges before the pills and patches did their work. But tonight the bracing did not help. The twinges got angry, louder, transforming themselves into waves. Harry couldn't take the waves. When he was younger, maybe. When his wife was alive and the kids lived at home, he could take it. Not anymore. He tried remembering when he had last changed his patch. He couldn't remember. His left thumb kept clicking.

His heart was pounding and he had sweated through the bedding now. He yanked off the old patch and replaced it, tearing the package open with his teeth. His left thumb kept clicking. The waves slowed down, but his panic had not. His breathing became rapid, erratic. He began gasping for air. He was drowning. His left thumb kept clicking. Finally, his breathing slowed and steadied. He needed a pill, he thought. It had been hours since the last pill. It seemed like hours. The hours ran together for Harry these days. He managed to get a second pill between his lips, but it did not go down his panic-dried throat so easily. His left thumb kept clicking.

The waves were gone, the twinges forgotten, even the hints were faded. Harry felt he could almost sleep. He passed the remote back into his right hand, but his right thumb was disinterested. Harry's lids flickered. He fought the urge to close them. Harry was afraid of sleep, but the fear was weak in him tonight. He clicked off the television and let his eyes close. Harry rolled over and let a pillow be his wife. In this twilight time, he laughed to himself that his wife had never been so thin as a pillow. It was good to pretend, though. And as he drifted off, Harry thought he could hear her call to him that she would protect him from the waves forever. With that promise, Harry's twilight was ended.

They were careless people, Tom and Daisy—they smashed up things and creatures and then retreated back into their money or vast carelessness, or whatever it was that kept them together, and let other people clean up the mess they had made.
—F. Scott Fitzgerald, *The Great Gatsby*

Damaged Goods

I turned to look over my left shoulder at MacClough seated two pews back. I didn't think it possible for a man to age so much in a month. He seemed thicker around the middle than I remembered. Four weeks hadn't lightened the blue of his eyes any, but that mischievous sparkle, though not gone, seemed dimmer somehow, smudged like old wax. His golden, surfer-dude hair had gone gray. Maybe it had been graying for years and I'd been blinded by close proximity. Maybe I hadn't wanted to see.

Johnny noticed my stare. His sad smile and signature wink told me so. They were gestures meant not to distract, but to acknowledge and give comfort. Sleight of hand was not MacClough's way. His wink let me know that he too had seen in the mirror the changes in him I was only noticing now. The smile. . . Well, the smile said many things. It said he knew I was hurting and that showing it was all right with him. But beyond that, it seemed to say that a funeral was no place to judge a man by his looks or to judge a man at all.

He was right, of course. Often, the only person at a funeral who seems at ease with him or herself is the body in the box. And today, not even that was true. My father was a stranger to me and, if he could have seen what they had done to his face, he would have felt a stranger to himself as well. It wasn't the vaudeville greasepaint—powders and rouges aren't, when all is said and done, very good understudies for coursing blood and muscle tone—that made him so alien. On the contrary, as he'd always had a maudlin love of clowns, the makeup was perversely appropriate. It was that they had shaved off his moustache. They shouldn't have done that. I didn't know him without that moustache.

My first impulse was anger. Anger is always my first impulse. It was my dad's legacy, anger. Anger is like an interesting mixture of black paint and acid. It blots out, erodes anything already on the canvas or on the pallet or in the heart. First, I wanted to slap the funeral directer: "For chrissakes! Who let the undertaker shave him?"

I slapped no one. I said nothing. Cowardice is the other half of the legacy.

Anger then turned to my brothers. How could they let him be shaved? But no one had asked their permission—"Excuse me, Mr. Klein, but would you like your dad's hair done in a shag cut? And that moustache. . . If you ask me, it's got to go!" I guess my brothers assumed, as I would have, that the whole world—okay, maybe not the whole world, but all of Brooklyn for sure—knew that Harry Klein always had a moustache. Always!

Finally, I directed my anger to where it would have gone anyway. I let it tear at me. Who was I to rage at anyone else? Where had I been when that twenty-five-cent razor was making a stranger of my dad? I'll tell you where I was. I was pitching, man, pitching. Four weeks in Los Angeles had schooled me in things the streets of Brooklyn never could. In Brooklyn, you learn to watch your back. In L.A., your back is the least of your worries.

Hollywood'd been my agent's idea: "The numbers on the book aren't so hot, but the artsy-fartsy types out there love it. You'll throw in a Latina partner for your detective and up the body count a little. . . . Don't worry."

He didn't let the fact that there was no screenplay bother him: "Who needs a screenplay? No screenplay means you're more flexible. You're not invested. They like flexible. Don't worry."

I should have worried. The first week we were out there, pitching my idea meant making a competently written detective novel with an arcane plot and surprise ending sound like the best investment since Microsoft. In week two it meant begging with dignity. By the third week it was just begging. By week four I'd taken to farting during meetings to get their attention. It was at the last of these performances that I'd gotten the call to come home. Suddenly, their attention mattered very little.

I nodded to MacClough and looked along the pew at my family. I took John's unspoken advice, trying not to judge them. My sisters-in-law seemed shaken down to their shoes. My brothers, on the other hand, appeared nearly catatonic. It was as if both their faces had been coated in a quick-setting

16

mortar, color-matached perfectly to their skins. But when you gazed closely enough, cracks showed in the plaster and there was an unmistakable redness in the folds of their eyes. Sometimes, tears themselves are unnecessary. My nieces and nephews were appropriately confused.

Zak, my brother Jeffrey's oldest son, was AWOL. Commitment to family was not high on my nephew's list of priorities. And as he seemed destined and determined to take up my mantle as the family fuck-up, his absence had not exactly set the world ablaze. No one was calling in the troops or printing Zak's likeness on milk cartons. I think he would have caused more of a ripple if he had just shown his face.

The rabbi began his routine. He was a man clearly inspired by the *Minute Waltz*. It had taken Harry Klein seventy-four years to live out his time, but the rabbi was intent upon summarizing them in as many seconds. I might not have minded the pace so much had he been able to muster some semblance of genuine feeling. He didn't have it in him. And when, twenty seconds into his tribute, the rabbi began buzz sawing through the third and fourth decades of my dad's life, I stopped listening and checked out the decor.

The chapel hadn't changed much since the service for my mother seven years earlier. It was only slightly more awful. There were faux bricks and faux beams and faded decals on the windows meant to give the appearance of stained glass. There was mylar wallpaper depicting scenes from the Old Testament and avocado cushions on the pews. With a splash of bad taxidermy you might mistake the place for a Hadassah hunting lodge.

Josh, the Klein brother with the misfortune of being born between Jeffrey and me, was up to do the eulogy. He said that he had found himself strangely ill-prepared for my father's passing. Me too, Josh. Me too. It was strange because we had been in dress rehearsal for his death since we could cross the street by ourselves. My dad had been stricken with a particularly insidious form of cancer. Excruciatingly painful and snail-like in growth, it killed him in pieces. Tenderness being one of the earliest casaulties. Harry Klein had collected scar tissue like some men col-

17

lected baseball memorabilia. He had averaged one surgical procedure for every year of my life. I would be glad to see that streak come to an end. Josh said just that. We would all be glad the pain was finally over.

I forced myself to look at the cherry-wood coffin that held those few pieces of my father that had not been divvied up between the surgeons and the sarcomas. For me, the doctors and the disease were two sides of the same coin: two gangs of clumsy thieves who had taken forever to make off with the goods. I remembered lying awake as a boy, praying for my father just to die. Some kids might have prayed for miracle cures, but even then I had dreadfully low expectations of the Almighty. But rather than killing off one embittered grocery clerk, God took the path of least resistance and murdered my faith instead. If my dad had died when I was young, I might've been able to imagine him as a man composed of something more than hard edges. In my fantasy, he might even have been capable of loving me back. As it was, I saw him much like I saw the dented and discounted cans he brought home from work. I saw him as he saw himself, as damaged goods.

At the cemetary, only the noise and backwash of passing jets prevented the rabbi from setting another speed record. I wondered if he kept a stopwatch in his pocket. When we finished taking turns at throwing our spadefuls of dirt on the coffin, people fractured into cliques. Talk turned to food. It's traditional for Jews; suffering and food. Aunt Lindy and Uncle Saul visited other graves. Their world had just gotten much smaller. Now they were the only two left from their generation.

"Whadya think of L.A.?" MacClough asked, squeezing my hand.

"I think Los Angelenos are lucky God feels bad about Sodom and Gomorrah."

"Terrible, huh?"

"Worse."

The preliminaries out of the way, we hugged. Our embrace saddened me more than I could say. Never once had my dad and I held each other in such an unselfconscious way. Surely now, we never would.

18

"Give me a ride back to Sound Hill?" I wondered.

"For a fee, my boy."

"I think I've got a spare quarter, you shanty Irish prick."

"Yeah, I missed you too, ya heathen Jew."

Jeffrey came away from one of the limousines and walked over to us. We hugged out of habit. Jeff's awkward embrace was not unlike my dad's.

"We need to talk," he said, taking a step back.

MacClough turned to go: "Meet you by my car."

"Stay," Jeffrey fairly commanded.

"I'll pass," Johnny kept going.

"No, please," Jeffrey insisted. "I want you to hear this."

To say that MacClough and my oldest brother were enemies would be an overstatement, but not much of one. Cops, even retired ones like Johnny, tend to develop a reflexive distaste for lawyers of Jeffrey's ilk. And Jeffrey's affection for the MacCloughs of this world was tepid at best.

"What is it, Jeff?"

"Zak's missing," he answered.

"Yeah," I said. "Par for the course."

Jeffrey shoved me. "You really are such an asshole, Dylan. Isn't it bad enough that he looks like you? Why does he have to put his parents through the same shit you pulled on Mom and Dad?"

There he was displaying the anger I was telling you about. But when I tried to display a little of my own, vice like fingers held back my left fist. John might have been weathering badly of late, but there wasn't a thing wrong with his grip.

"What do you mean he's missing?" MacClough asked, putting himself between Jeffrey and me.

"Let go of my arm!"

He didn't. "Shut up and let your brother talk."

Jeffrey opened his mouth to speak and stopped when he noticed the three of us had attracted a wee bit too much attention. Even Rabbi Rocketmouth let himself be distracted. MacClough let go of me and we all just stood there smiling like a trio of fools. When everyone realized there would be nothing more to see, they let us out of their sights.

"Do you still own that bar?" Jeffrey asked MacClough.

19

"The last I looked, yeah."

"What time do you close tonight?"

"Don't worry about when I close," Johnny said. "I'll see that it's slow when we need it to be."

"Thank you." Jeffrey about-faced.

"Don't forget your investigator's file," I called after him.

"How'd you know—" he started.

"I know you, Jeff. That's all I need to know. You would never come to me first."

He walked on. He was scared. And now, so was I.

Three Legs

Sound Hill is an old whaling village out toward the end of Long Island, some eighty miles east of the New York City line. George Washington never slept here, but he built us a clapboard lighthouse. It's got a bronze plaque on it and everything. We've got local Indians. We've got potato farms, sod farms, vineyards, and wineries. We've got several Victorian mansions, some shotgun shacks, but no high ranches. That pretty much sets us apart from the rest of Long Island. Sound Hill—The Last Bastion of High Ranch-lessness West of the Atlantic. But what we were proudest of was our lack of a golf course. That was us.

The Rusty Scupper, on Dugan Street off the marina, had been the only bar in town for a hundred years when MacClough bought it. He had owned it for two years when I moved my office from the City to a room above the bookstore. Sound Hill needed an insurance investigator about as much as it needed a greenskeeper, but I moved here anway. Business was bad in Brooklyn, I hated high ranches, and I wasn't much of an investigator. If I had a company motto, it would have read: *If you want mediocrity, you want me.* I think I'm maybe one of the eight people in history who actually believed he'd make more money as a writer. Luckily, I convinced a few editors.

Jeffrey, on the other hand, was Jeffrey. Operating according to some master plan the rest of us mere mortals were not privy to, Jeffrey acted like an escapee from the cast of *Götterdämmerung*. I have never been one to subscribe to the axiom that you can't argue with success, but my brother's list of achievements did make argument a difficult proposition. Summa cum laude at NYU, editor of the law review at Columbia, top litigator at Marx, O'Shea and Dassault, a seven-figure income, a beautiful wife, two healthy kids, and five acres overlooking the Hudson River, Jeffrey had reached about as high as most men dare to dream. If only he could have managed to tone down his imperious manner, I might have been able to share the same room with him for more than ten minutes. Don't misunderstand, Jeff was my big brother and I loved him. I admired him in ways I could not express. I only wished I liked him a little more and loved him a little less.

MacClough was true to his word without trying. During the summer, when Sound Hill enjoyed a modest seasonal boom and benefited from the Hamptons' overflow, the line at the Scupper's bar would have been three deep at 9:30. Such was not the case during the last week of February. The locals were all done with their Budweisers by 8:00. The college crowd was all dart-and-eight-balled out by 9:00.

Johnny and I had earlier agreed that we would not waste our energies speculating about Zak. We were both sure that Jeffrey's news would be taxing enough without us helping it along any. A few minutes before my brother's scheduled arrival, MacClough put Patsy Cline on the juke and began rumbling around under the bar out of my sight. He only ever played Patsy when he was thinking about lost loves or absent friends. That was the thing about her voice, it just ached. And she always sounded as if she knew the next hurt was never more than a breath away.

Johnny reappeared. He put two glasses on the bar next to as fine a crystal bottle as I had every seen. It was nearly empty. Still, he poured two amber fingers full in each glass and waited for Patsy to finish her lament.

"Amen, Patsy. Amen." He bowed his head. "Klein! Get your flat Jewish ass over to this bar."

"What?"

"Do you know what this is?" MacClough pointed at the decanter as I came his way.

"Holy shit!" I could be so articulate. "That's the Napoleon brandy your father—"

"—pinched from the dead bootlegger. That's right, Klein. You remember. But I bet you a fin you don't remember the bootlegger's name."

"Izzy Three Legs Weinstein," I said without missing a beat.

Raising his glass: "Screw ya, ya Christ-killer. To your dad!"

"I hate brandy."

"It's the only proper way to send a man to meet his god."

"You say the same thing when they polish the plaque on the lighthouse: 'It's the only proper way to celebrate the cleaning of the plaque'."

"Klein!"

"John, I just can't," I was serious now. "There's hardly another drink left in that bottle. You shouldn't waste it on me. It's part of your family."

"So are you, you idiot. Drink."

"To Harry Klein!" I knocked it back. "Feh."

"Feh?"

"All due respect to family heirlooms, French emperors, and deceased bootleggers, but I can't stand the stuff."

"Fuckin' neanderthal," he chided and slapped a five-dollar bill on the bar. "Here's the fin I owe you."

I folded it up and slipped it into my jacket pocket next to the black skullcap from the funeral home. I don't know why, but I hadn't showered or changed clothes since getting off the plane that morning. The tops of my shoes were still powered with souvenir dirt from the grave site. When I looked up from my shoes, the crystal decanter and brandy glasses were gone. In their stead were a Black and Tan and a double of Old Bushmills.

I went for my pint: "To Three Legs and five dollars!"

Jeff walked in at precisely the wrong time.

"If you're this convivial on the day we bury your father and discover your nephew is missing, you must be a scream on good days."

"You've got it all wrong, counselor," MacClough jumped to my defense.

"No, Mr. MacClough, I have it all right. I know my little brother."

"Get to the point, Jeffrey," I said. "What about Zak?"

He tossed a manila folder on the bar. MacClough grabbed it and skimmed through it as Jeffrey spoke.

"Zak didn't call home the week before February break. We weren't particularly alarmed. He's nearly as irresponsible as his Uncle Dylan used to be."

"Fuck you, Jeff. Just fuck—"

MacClough threw his Bushmills past my ear. It landed

23

the hard way on the cobbles of the old fireplace. The flying glass got our attention.

"Either start acting more like brothers and less like a married couple or get the fuck out of me pub. Got it Klein?"

"Got it."

"Counselor?" MacClough asked.

"Understood."

"Go on then with what you've got to say, counselor."

"Even when he didn't show at home the Friday evening of his break week, Tess and I weren't worried. It wouldn't have been the first time."

"Yeah," MacClough smirked. "I got that impression."

"But by late that Sunday," Jeff continued, "I was concerned. Tess too. To allay her fears I told her that Zak and I had a falling out over his schoolwork and that by not showing he was just acting out."

"I take it your wife had no problem believing you."

"No problem at all, Mr. MacClough. In the meantime, I called around to his friends and roommates. No one seemed to know anything. I made some discreet inquiries through a close business associate who is a well-connected alum of Riversborough."

"Zak goes to Riversborough College," I said for no good reason. "Upstate, by the Canadian border."

"I figured that out, Klein." Turning to Jeff: "Any help?"

"None," my brother sighed. "The next morning I went to the Castle-on-Hudson Police and reported Zak missing."

"No ransom notes? No threatening phone calls?"

"I sort of wish there were," Jeff said. "Then I'd have something to hold onto. I had to tell Tess eventually, but Zaks's younger brother Lindsay doesn't know."

"He knows," I said. "Maybe not all the details, but he knows. How's Tess holding up?"

"She's the strongest person I ever met. Until this thing with Dad, she barely showed any cracks. When the police came up empty, I hired Hench Security. That's a copy of their case file to date."

"Hench?" I puzzled.

"They're good," MacClough assured me. "All ex-FBI and ATF agents. They're also supposed to have a few cyber-

24

geeks from the NSA on the payroll. But I thought their forte was industrial security, not missing persons."

"So far, your assessment is correct. They've interviewed everyone but Lee Harvey Oswald's wife and gotten no further than the Castle-on-Hudson police."

"Have you called the papers?" I wondered.

"No press, for chrissakes! No press!"

"So," John wanted to know, "what is it exactly that you expect me and your brother to do that the cops and the Mission Impossible crew can't?"

"Though thankfully retired from fraud investigation, my brother Dylan isn't an amateur and will know how to stay out of your way. On the other hand, he loves Zak and won't be inclined to let you take chances with my son's life that a law enforcement agency or security firm might be willing to risk. He and Zak also share a certain unspoken affinity, a sixth sense for what the other is thinking."

"That's right," I said, "it takes one fuck-up to know another."

"Shut up, Klein," MacClough scolded. "Keep going, counselor."

"I've always resented Zak and Dylan's closeness, but now maybe some good can come of it. If Zak is close by, my brother will know it."

MacClough wasn't buying it. "That's a good case for your brother's involvement, but where do I fit in with the Klein family psychic network?"

"I've been checking up on you, Dectective."

"Retired."

Jeffrey ignored that. "I've also been reading your personnel file from the NYPD."

"That's confidential!" Johnny screamed, red in the face, veins popping out of his neck.

"Come on, detective. Don't play dumb. In a city like New York, nothing is confidential, nothing is off-limits, especially to people like me. You know that."

"Yeah," MacClough said, pouring himself a double, "I know. It sucks, but I know."

"Yes, I should think after the Hernandez case you'd be well acquainted with the vagaries and benefits of the system."

"All right, counselor, you made your point." MacClough downed his drink in one gulp. "Leave the file. Your brother and me will be up to see the Castle-on-Hudson PD tomorrow morning. Do me a favor, don't let 'em know we're coming. If they're like most cops, they resent the shit out of people who they think expect special treatment. The fact that you're a lawyer also works against you."

"It's in your hands," Jeffrey smiled, just briefly. He couldn't help celebrating a victory even if his son's life was in danger. "I won't insult you by offering payment now, but I've transferred $25,000 into Dylan's bank account for your use. I don't care what you do with it. You don't have to account for it. If you require more, you'll get more within a minute of the phone call. All I want is Zak back safely."

"You know, counselor," John said, "I would have helped just on Dylan's behalf. Why bring Hernandez into it?"

"When it comes to motivation, Detective, I believe in overkill. Good night." He took a step to go, then stopped and looked me in the eye. "I've already made excuses for your absence at *shivah*."

"Oh yeah?" I was incredulous. "What did you tell them?"

"That you sold your screenplay and had to go back to L.A. Maybe when Zak's home, you will go back."

"I doubt it, but let's find Zak first."

Jeffrey was gone. And before I got the name Hernandez out of my mouth, MacClough shooed me out of the Scupper. I had to change. I had to shower. I had to get some rest, he said. We had a long day ahead of us. He had to read through the file. He had to find someone to cover for him at the bar. He had a thousand things to do before tomorrow.

By the time my wet hair landed on my pillow for the first time in a month, I had almost forgotten about Hernandez. Almost.

Lovesong Lane

We were two hours and three cups of coffee into the trip, just crossing the Tappan Zee, when MacClough began giving instructions. I was to do most of the talking, at least in the beginning. I was just a concerned uncle who had asked an old friend along for the long ride. Johnny would pick his spot and take over, but I was always to stand between him and the investigating detective. John threw the Hench Security file on my lap and told me to look through it. I did.

MacClough was right, Hench was thorough. Not only did the file contain verbatim transcripts of all their interviews, bios, and background material on the interviewees, but there was a copy of the Castle-on-Hudson Police Department report and bios of the investigating officers. It was all so precise and the binding wasn't bad either. Unfortunately, neither Hench nor the police nor any of Zak's friends had any idea of his whereabouts or, if they had, they weren't saying.

"So," Johnny broke the quiet a few minutes out of town, "how you holding up?"

"Like a straw man."

"Then we'll have to keep you outta the wind."

"Last night, my brother mentioned the Hernan—"

"You know," he cut me off, "last night after you left, I couldn't help thinking about the last time I saw my old man. He was in the hospital and he whispers in my ear to get rid of the nurse. When I do, he pulls out two cans of Rheingold from under his damned pillow."

"No shit! What'd'y do?"

"I laid into him good."

"Why, because he wasn't allowed to drink?"

"No, Klein, because the beer was warm. We never shared much, me and the old man, but at least we shared that Rheingold."

After a pause, I said: "You know my brother's not telling us everything."

"I know. I just can't figure out what he's holding back

or why. When he got so determined about no press involvement, I knew something wasn't kosher. We're here!"

Castle-on-Hudson had once been the exclusive enclave
of old moneyed families whose names read like the passenger manifest from the *Mayflower*. These days, the locals
were more apt to be descended from peasants that sailed
across the Atlantic in steerage. The most recent arrivals,
however, tended to migrate on 747s owned by Air India or
All Nippon Air. Still, the majority of lots were zoned for a
minimum of two acres and handyman specials went for
about half a million.

The police station was an old stone building that looked
like a set piece from *MacBeth*. The police department itself
was the typically schizophrenic kind of force you find in
wealthy communities. The uniformed officers tended to be
young, obedient muscle-heads who liked to write tickets and
carry 9 mms. Armed meter maids, MacClough called them.
The detectives were a whole 'nother story. They were
mostly retired big city detectives. Some just missed the job.
Some were looking for a second pension. They were well
paid and happy not have to deal with the bureaucratic bullshit big city departments serve up in large portions. If
MacClough were inclined, he'd have been an ideal candi-
date.

No one seemed to pay us much mind as we walked
through the front doors. There was a flurry of activity in the
station house. Packs of uniformed officers ran up and down
the twin spiral staircases that stood to either side of the main
desk. To our right, three stony-faced state troopers studied a
local map. To our left, a small horde of media types waited
impatiently outside the police chief's door.

"What's going on?" I asked Johnny. "I mean, I've never
been in here before, but I can't imagine that Castle-on-
Hudson usually attracts much press. And what are the state
troopers doing?"

"I don't—" he cut himself off as we approached the main
desk. "See the black band across the sergeant's badge?"

"Dead cop?"

"Dead cop, probably murdered. The press doesn't turn
out for kidney failure." He crossed himself. "Let's just do

28

what we came here to do. You remember the detective's name, right?"

"Caliparri, retired member of the Detective Bureau of the Newark, New Jersey Police Department."

"Good."

The desk sergeant didn't exactly snap to attention when we approached. That was fine with me. It gave me more time to study the soft lines of her face and imagine how her pulled-back auburn hair might fall against her lightly freckled skin. When she looked up, the corners of her full lips smiled politely, but the corners of her eyes smiled not at all. Eyes shot with blood are never easy to look at. The blue shine of her eyes made the contrast even harder to take.

"How can I help you gentlemen?" she asked, her voice cracking slightly.

"Detective Caliparri?" She went pale. "Your names?"

"Dylan Klein. John MacClough."

"One moment." She picked up the phone, punched in a few numbers, and turned her back to us. We could hear her whisper, but not her words. With some color having returned to her cheeks, she faced us and said: "Staircase to your right. One flight up, third door to your left."

"Thank you, Sergeant. . .Hurley," I read off her name tag. "Sorry for your loss."

She just bowed her head and waved us up the steps.

*   *   *

"Come," the answer came to my knock.

By the time MacClough closed the door behind us, my clothes needed washing. The place reeked of cigarettes and a layer of smoke hung in midair like a sleeping ghost. A man, trying hard to look disinterested, sat on the corner of a desk smoking a Kent. He had a kind, meaty face with a nose that twisted more ways than a ski trail. He was dark-skinned, gray-haired, and brown-eyed. His smoke-yellowed fingers were thick and square at the nail. When he finally stopped the disinterested act, he looked right past me: "John MacClough." His voice was raspy. His tone was equal parts anger and disdain.

"Klein," Johnny said, "meet Detective Nick Fazio, late of the NYPD."

I shook his hand. He shook back. Whatever Fazio had against MacClough apparently wasn't going to be held against me.

"Look," I said, "it's nice that you guys go back. I'm all for reunions, but I'm here to talk to Detective Caliparri."

"Then I guess you're gonna have to hold a seance. Caliparri's dead. Someone broke into his house last night and decided to give him a haircut with a shotgun."

"Robbery?" MacClough wanted to know.

"The place was ransacked," Fazio answered, "but the perp left a few grand in cash and jewelery untouched. So whatever he was there for, it wasn't money. What did you want to talk to him about Mr. Klein?"

"My nephew, Zak Klein. My older brother reported him—"

"Here it is!" Fazio pulled a folder off his desk, waved it at me, stopped and read through it. He looked up and flicked his cigarette butt at MacClough's feet. "So you're Jeffrey Klein's brother."

"I have that dubious distinction," I confessed.

"So now I understand why you're here, sort of. What's his excuse?"

"He's a close family friend."

"Really!" Fazio stood, walked by me, and got right in MacClough's face. "Geez, and I thought it might have something to do with Hernandez, this being a missing kid and all."

There was that name again, Hernandez. Ten years we'd known each other and the name Hernandez had only come up in relation to Mets' baseball. Now, two days in a row, it surfaces in connection with one of MacClough's cases. Weird. Over the past decade, I thought I'd heard every lurid detail of every big case—good and bad—involving John MacClough. Apparently, one case had slipped his mind. It hadn't, however, slipped the minds of Jeff Klein or Nick Fazio. On the contrary, the Hernandez case seemed like a very hot topic.

"Show the man some respect, Fazio," MacClough said

coolly. "His nephew is missing and he buried his old man yesterday. You think he gives a shit about us?"

"Sorry about your father," the detective said, finally facing me. "Look, Mr. Klein, I know the file. I'll tell you what Caliparri probably told that big *macher* brother of yours; the kid split. Maybe the pressure of school got too much for him. Maybe he knocked up some girl. Maybe it's drugs, maybe booze. Maybe it's all of the above. In this town, the major cash crop is dysfunctional teenagers. Money fucks 'em up. Now don't get me wrong. We'll keep the file open, but he'll show of his own accord. In this town, they always do."

I wanted to argue. I didn't. He made sense. I hoped like hell he was right. I peeked over my shoulder at MacClough, but his expression said nothing to me.

"Thank you, Detective. I hope you don't mind if I check in with you every few days."

"Not at all, Mr. Klein. Sorry again about your dad."

"Sorry about Detective Caliparri," I said.

He was too busy lighting up to respond. I was by the door, but MacClough had yet to move. He seemed distant, preoccupied.

"Do you think they're related?" MacClough spoke to Fazio.

"Is what related," the detective asked rhetorically, "a dead cop and a missing college boy? You been off the job too long. They happened weeks apart. And you're forgetting, technically the kid went missing all the way the hell upstate in Riversborough. What's the connection?"

"Just a thought," MacClough said, "just a thought."

As I began pulling Fazio's office door open, someone on the other side pushed it hard. That displeased my right knee greatly.

"Sorry!" It was Sergeant Hurley.

"For chrissakes, Hurley, what is it?" Fazio was impatient.

"Private security firm reports a 1030."

"Call out the fucking National Guard!" Impatience turned to sarcasm. "I got a dead cop here. On a good day I

31

don't give a rat's ass about a 1030. What makes today any different?"

"I think it's kinda relevant," Hurley sneered.

"Why? Where'd the break-in happen, at the mayor's residence?"

"No Detective Fazio, it happened at 5 Lovesong Lane. That's Mr.—"

I cut her off. "That's my brother's house!"

Either Zak's room had been ripped apart by someone who had a grudge against electronic equipment and wallboard or it had been visited by the world's most discerning tornado. It even looked worse than most teenagers' rooms. The rest of Jeffrey's Victorian nirvana up there overlooking the Hudson had remained untouched.

Before we went in, MacClough said just this: "You know nothing."

That was a pretty accurate assessment, I thought. But I knew what he meant. Insurance investigators play this game with police all the time. I was to keep private anything I might notice. Fazio and his uniformed minions were to be frozen out, at least for the time being. It was especially easy to play the game that day, for, as I kept reminding the local constabulary: I didn't live there. I didn't know where things went. I didn't know what was missing. It got so tedious, I wanted to run to the nearest print shop and have cards made that read: "My brother will be here shortly. Ask him!"

MacClough had kept his mouth shut until Fazio, frustrated with my inconvenient lack of knowledge and my ban on his smoking in Jeffrey's house, dismissed us: "You can go."

"Still think there's no connection?" MacClough wondered aloud.

"What I think is police business and you ain't police, not anymore."

"Same M.O. as Caliparri minus the body?" MacClough guessed.

"Same answer as before. Only now, I'm ordering you to leave."

When John sensed that I was going to argue, he pulled me out of the house by the arm. He may have been on bad terms with Fazio, but apparently it was important to maintain some measure of goodwill with the detective.

"Where we going?" I asked as we walked to his old Thunderbird.

"I'm not going anywhere."

"And me?"

"You're going to college."

Long Sleeves

The cab fare back to Sound Hill was roughly equivalent to
one quarter of the advance to my first book. God knows, I
wrote the damned thing in less time than it took to get home.
I stopped by the Scupper to pass on a few instructions from
MacClough to his brother Billy and to wash the day down
with a pint. One pint turned into two and two into three.
Billy gave me a lift after I helped him close the place.

Procrastination time was over once I'd showered and
shaved. I went to my writing desk and dug out Larry Feld's
business card. I flipped the card over to where he'd written
down his home number. I punched in the numbers and half
prayed to get his answering machine.

Larry Feld was sort of a lawyer from the dark side of the
force. Stated politely, Larry was an attorney who represented outcasts, societal pariahs, and miscreants. In fact, he
was a Mafia lawyer who defended the occasional serial
rapist or pedophile. But Larry Feld was also a guy who'd
grown up on my block, a guy who used to invite me over for
Passover seder. He had gotten me my first jobs as an investigator and always made sure to feed me enough work to pay
the bills. Problem with Larry Feld was, he never did anything out of the goodness of his heart. It was a toss-up as to
whether he just didn't understand goodness or had no heart.
The jury was still out. What Larry did understand was the
system and what he did have was connections. He was not
unlike my brother Jeffrey in those respects. If you needed
information, he could get it. The bill, however, was almost
always too steep.

"What is it?" He was home.

"It's Dylan, Larry."

"Sorry about your dad."

"How the fuck did you—"

"One hears things. I sent a basket," he said. "Your dad
always hated my guts. At least he wasn't a phony about it
and he treated my folks with respect."

Feld's parents had survived Auschwitz, but not at all
intact. His father was a morose little man who wore long

sleeves on dog days to hide as many scars as he could. His mother painted their windows black. For cruel children and their crueler parents, the Felds were easy targets for every joke and whisper.

"Thanks," I said. "He did hate you."

"Enough sweet talk, Dylan. You only call me when you want something."

"Hernandez and Fazio. Hernandez is an NYPD case that could go back maybe twenty, thirty years. John MacClough had some involvement in it. Fazio is a dectective up in Castle-on-Hudson. Used to be NYPD."

"Hernandez I've got to look into. If Fazio's first name is Nick, I can give you something now."

"Nick's the name," I confirmed.

"Most decorated detective to ever work Internal Affairs. Retired, detective first grad. He's got a great rep. Even the guys he brought down respect him. Works in Castle-on-Hudson to prove to the world he's real cop, not just another cheese eater."

"See if Fazio and MacClough intersect at Hernandez."

"Shit!" he hissed. "You don't need me. You need a road map."

"I need you, Larry. Trust me."

"You're the only the person I know who could say that and get away with it. Give me two days."

When Larry clicked off the line, I began dialing my father's number. Old habits are harder to bury than the dead.

They Don't Play Stickball in Milwaukee

The airport at Riversborough was the stuff of sketch comedy. Though situated just south of the Canadian border, it wasn't exactly a major hub. It had one runway, a wind sock, and a terminal building the size of a Photomat. None of this, however, prevented the port authority from shamelessly proclaiming: "Welcome to Riversborough International Airport—The best little gateway this side of the border." I would have hated to see the worst little gateway.

Snow and liberal arts were Riversborough's major commodities. As I drove my rental into town, I read several billboards for the area ski resorts. They all, apparently, liked the copywriter for the local port authority. Their ads were equally shameless and catagorically featured the words best and little. I wasn't great at Scrabble, but I bet I could have kicked that copywriter's ass.

When I checked in with the local police, they gave me the same song and dance Fazio had laid on me, only in a more polite, northern New York kind of way. Zak would turn up. They were sure of it. None of them had attended the college, but they knew it was extremely competitive. And when one cop told me that Riversborough was the best little liberal arts college town in the east, I asked him if he had any relatives in advertising.

The campus was postcard pretty. The buildings were all red brick and white clapboards bordering a central quadrangle. The only bit of ostentation was the gold dome atop the library clock tower. There was no visible activity on campus and a visitor might suspect school was still in recess. But like many schools situated in snow belts, underground tunnels connected all the buildings.

I parked in the visitors' lot and made my way around to the dorms. Though not quite as quaint as the main body of the campus, their design features were consistent with the rest of the school's architecture. When I walked up to Zak's door there was already someone waiting. Her nature was a mystery to me as she rested her head on her knees and hugged her blue-jeaned legs.

"How ya doing?"

She was startled. "God, you sound like Zak."

"People say that."

After inspecting my face, she said: "You look like him too."

"People say he looks like me. I'm his Uncle—"

"—Dylan." She popped up and shook my hand. "Way cool. Zak talks about you all the time. You're the cop turned writer."

"Something like that." I was happy to hear her refer to Zak in the present tense. "And you are?"

"Oh, sorry. Kira, Kira Wantanabe." She bowed slightly.

Kira Wantanabe made my heart pound. I couldn't imagine a man whose heart wouldn't pound at the sight of her. I let go of her hand, afraid she might feel my palm begin to moisten. We just stood there for a second, smiling awkwardly at one another.

"Do you know where Zak is?" I finally got to the point.

"I wish I did. Like I told the cops and those other men, he just split a few days before break and I haven't seen him since. I come up here at this time every day to see if he's back." She frowned.

"Are you two. . .I mean. . ." Jesus, I sounded like a jerk.

"No, Uncle Dylan," Kira smiled coyly, "we are not. Last year we were together once. We are happier as friends." She checked her watch. "I have class."

"Can we talk later, please?"

"Yes, I would like to speak to you. Meet me in front of the library at 7:00. Great." She bowed again, ever so slightly.

I watched her move in silence down the hall.

I opened the door to Zak's room with a key Jeffrey had provided. One of the advantages, some might say disadvantages, of Riversborough was that students were not required to double up. Zak had chosen to live alone. It was probably a mistake and it was probably my fault. In our talks, I used to prattle on about how living for years by myself was the best thing I had ever done. It teaches you about confronting loneliness. It teaches you about responsibility. You learn the downside of freedom. It never occured to me that he would listen. I guess I forgot to mention that I waited until after college to start down my solitary path.

When I stepped inside I noticed that Zak's Riversborough room had the same nouveau tornado look as his room at home. Someone was searching very hard for something he was convinced my nephew possessed. And whatever this guy lacked in the way of delicacy, he more than compensated for with raw determination. I put a call in to the best little police department this side of the border.

The music remained the same, but there were variations on the lyrics. The Riversborough cops were still sure that nothing was wrong with Zak. They were sure another student had noticed Zak gone and took advantage of the situation.

MacClough wasn't too terribly surprised by the news. He said he would have been more shocked if Zak's dorm room had been left untouched. He made me write down some questions for Kira Wantanbe. I asked what was going on on his end. He said he was reinterviewing as many of the Castle-on-Hudson friends as he could, but that all it had gotten him so far was a couple of cups of herbal tea and several dirty looks. He had one or two more friends to check out before calling it a night. He was staying up at Jeffrey's place. Fazio had located a safe-deposit box key at Caliparri's house, but couldn't be at all sure it had anything to do with Zak's disappearance or Caliparri's murder. Fazio was going to track down the bank and get a subpoena.

"Wait a second," I said. "What did you and Fazio do, kiss and make up or something? How do you know so much about what he's doing?"

"Sergeant Hurley's been helpful."

"How did you get to her?"

"I didn't," he said. "She came to me."

"That old MacClough charm strikes again."

"It's not me she's interested in, Klein. Can I help it if she's got no taste in men?"

"Fuck you very much. Later."

"After noon. Maybe I'll have something."

*　　*　　*

It had begun to snow as I made my way across campus. Once again, Kira Wantanabe was waiting. She didn't notice me right away, so I stood in the shadows watching the white flakes landing on her lush black hair that fell well below the shoulders of her coat. She was slender as a blade of grass and not much taller than five feet, but she stood strong against the wind. The sharp lines of her calf muscles showed themselves through her thick wool leggings. Under the light, the skin of her triangular face was milky and translucent all at once like the outer layer of a pearl.

When I stepped out of the shadows, we shook hands nervously and for too long. She smiled broadly and then, embarrassed by what it might have said to me, she made it disappear.

"Come on," she said and led me off campus.

We did not talk. I was glad for that. I felt tongue-tied and awkward and seventeen all over again. I could smell her hair: jasmine blooming in the snow. It was odd that this girl should make me feel alive. It had been a while. My internal voice kept reminding me about Zak and my father and Detective Caliparri, but after several hundred yards all I could hear was our footsteps.

The coffeehouse was downstairs, dark, and smelled like Fazio's office. There was graffiti and drip paintings on the walls. Some clown in a beret was playing the bongos, snapping his fingers, reciting "Beat lite" poetry. It wasn't half bad but I was willing to bet he knew the lyrics to Pearl Jam songs far better than he knew Mexico City Blues or Howl. It was kind of fun, but facade. It was a fashion for the college kids to try on and discard like miniskirts or love beads. Next year it would be a disco.

I ordered an Irish coffee. Kira ordered tea. When the waitress left our drinks, Kira pulled something out from her bag and laid it on the table near the candle.

"I hope you don't mind," she hid her face, "but could you sign this for me?"

It was a dog-eared copy of my last book—the one I couldn't sell as a screenplay—*They Don't Play Stickball In Milwaukee.* Too hard-boiled for the 90s, the critics said. Too hard-boiled, my ass.

When I hesitated, she panicked a bit. "I'm sorry, I shouldn't have asked. Please—"

"Don't be silly," I said and took her pen.

She read the inscription: "'Dear Kira, Skin of pearls. Jasmine blooming in the snow.' It's beautiful. I don't understand it, but it's beautiful."

"Maybe sometime you will understand."

She leaned across the table and kissed me on the cheek. "I like the way your beard feels."

"The kiss didn't feel too shabby."

She put the book back in her bag. We ordered more drinks. She had an Irish coffee this time. The waitress carded her. Good thing Kira carried the requisite fake ID. It had been several decades since I'd had a drink with a coed below drinking age. Her attentiveness, enthusiasm, not to mention her physical beauty, all appealed to my vanity. And at forty, my vanity had grown small, weak.

I asked her MacClough's questions to no avail. She knew more about Jimmy Hoffa's disappearance than Zak's. Johnny and I had only been at it for two days, but it was getting to the point where a dead end might've seemed encouraging. Kira was good about not asking too many questions I could not or would not answer. She sensed, I guess, my unwillingness to go in that direction.

"I'm an English Literature major, you know." She was quick to change subjects. "I love writing, but I can't write. Too much loneliness. Too much looking inside."

"You know a lot about loneliness, do you?"

"Yes." There was an uncomfortable silence. "So, what's it like to be a published author?"

"The fantasy's a lot better than the reality. Mainly, getting published helps you get in touch with your own obscurity." She frowned. That wasn't the answer she wanted to hear. "I'm sorry," I said. "I'm out of sorts and lonely. Lonely is okay when I'm home at my desk writing. Here . . ."

"I understand." Kira put her face very close to mine. "Where are you staying?"

"The Old Watermill Inn. Why?"

"Because, Uncle Dylan, there is nothing obscure about you and I want to chase our demons together tonight."

I had no argument to make that would have convinced either one of us she was wrong.

The World Did Spin

I lie in the dark listening to the faint hiss of the hotel shower. There is a red-and-yellow neon light flashing through the blinds. I'm up now, an unfiltered Camel dangles from my lips. Reaching into my suit jacket, I come away with a pint bottle wrapped in brown paper. I break the government seal with a twist and take a bracer of the cheap hooch. It goes down smooth as a mouthful of cut glass. I take another swig. The glass is still cut, but the edges aren't as sharp. I unholster my .38 and spin the cylinder just because I enjoy the clicking sound it makes. I press my ear against the bathroom door. The shower's still going. I unclasp her handbag and use the barrel of the .38 to poke around. Never know what a frail might carry in there that'll jump up and bite you. But this one's smart. There's nothing to let me know the real motive for her sharing my bed. The water's off. I clasp the bag, replace it. I holster my piece and pour some of the liquor into the glass marked with the come-and-get-it silhouette of her painted lips. She steps back into the bedroom, towel wrapped just above her pink nipples. I hand her the glass, saying: "I missed you."

"Well," she says, "I had to give you enough time to go through my bag, didn't I?"

"You're smart, angel, very smart."

As she reaches for the glass, the towel falls conveniently to the floor. The smart talk stops there.

*　　　*　　　*

Of course, there was no neon sign. There was nothing remotely neon about Riversborough. And though I lay in bed listening to the hiss of the shower, distracting myself with pulp clichés, all I could think about was that slender blade of glass.

She had been remarkably shy, not coy, not virginal. She did not want light. And there in the blackness, we moved slowly. Kira removed my clothes, marking her progress with gentle kisses. There was no clawing, no fury. It was ritual.

Her clothes fell away without much urging. I took hold of her at the back of her thighs and pulled her weightless body up along my torso. Her breasts were smallish and firm. I held her nipple between my teeth and used the tip of my tongue to tease it hard. She purred, clutching at the back of my neck, wrapping her legs above my waist. She began to roll the nipple of her other breast between her own fingers.

"Please! Please! Please!" She stiffened, shuddered, shuddered again.

I could feel moisture pouring out of her, meandering through the hair on my abdomen. She released herself and slid down my body washing her orgasm off me with her tongue. She took me into her mouth and I exploded almost immediately. I might have in any case, even without physical encouragement on her part. She braced herself against my thighs, struggling to take it all in. I fell back on the bed and for the first time in a long time, I remembered that the world did spin.

"I knew," she whispered in the darkness, "that I would love your taste."

"How long have you known?"

"Later," she said, "I will show you."

She crawled up onto the bed next to me. She coaxed my hand onto the sparse, wet hair of her pubis. I massaged her clitoris and as I felt her muscles tense, I slid my finger down hard inside her. Kira clamped her hands around my wrist and held my hand in place until the waves had fully passed. When she relaxed, I pulled my hand up to my mouth and licked her off my finger. She licked, too. I wanted more and moved my mouth along soft skin until I picked up the taste of jasmine mixing with something raw, untamed and mildly bitter.

That was . . . Jesus, I don't know. I wasn't keeping time. I wanted to join her in the shower, but she resisted. She said she liked the scent of sex on a man. I was stunned by her, by her skillful blend of ritual and spontaneity. I had never been with a woman so understanding of her partner, so aware of herself and so young. It was an addictive combination to a man with as many miles on him as I had. She had the rare ability to make the few seconds leading up to orgasm more exciting than the orgasm itself. It was no wonder that Zak was intimidated by her. At nineteen I was so unsure, so inexperienced that I wanted to jump out of my own skin. I would have been completely overmatched by a woman like Kira. I was overmatched now.

As I waited for her to return to my bed, I wondered if Zak had been embarrassed by Kira, if he still hurt when he thought about her. I wondered if he was all right. I fell asleep wondering.

*   *   *

I felt her slide herself around me as I opened my eyes. Light crept in through the shade, but it was so diffuse that it did not blind me. My vision was grainy, faded like a blowup from a cheap photo lab. Her back was to me, riding slowly, the muscles of her vagina tight against me. I lay back for a minute and let her ride. I reached up and ran my fingers through her thick, straight, ebony hair. It was frighteningly like silk, too perfect.

"Pull it!" she demanded, picking up her pace. "Pull it! Make it hurt!"

As I pulled, I got an eerie feeling that I had done this before. I hadn't. Believe me, I would remember. But I couldn't escape the familiarity of the scene. There was a resonance in her words, even in the way she rode me.

"That's it!" she sighed. "Harder!"

I pulled harder. She quickened the pace. She reached back, taking my right hand, and guided it onto her right nipple. I pinched it, but not too hard. She gasped. Her back muscles flexed erratically. Her thighs began to stiffen. And as they did, another wave of resonance passed through me. My head was swimming, fighting to keep one part of itself uninvolved. Was I losing it completely? *Had* I done this before?

"Harder!" she repeated. "Pinch it! Pinch it!"

I sat up some and placed my left index finger on the moving target of her clitoris. When I found it, Kira wrapped her hand around my finger and rubbed herself. We rubbed together, fast and faster. We were very close now. I waited for her to start crying: "Please! Please! Please!" But that cry never came.

"That's it, lover," she sang. "That's it! Hard—er. Hard—er.'"

Breathless, she could barely speak the words. And again the words, even the intonations were familiar to me. But how?

"Oh God, Wyatt! Wyatt! Wyatt!" she screamed, stiffened around me, and shook so fiercely the bed moved. "Wyatt."

As I writhed in orgasm beneath her, the confusion vanished. Wyatt Rosen was my character, the detective featured in my two novels: *Coney Island Burning* and *They Don't Play Stickball in Milwaukee*. In *They Don't Play*, Wyatt Rosen hooks up with a newspaper reporter named Anne Curtis. In an attempt to gain insight into Rosen's investigation of an allegedly corrupt Wisconsin congressman—a transplanted Brooklynite, hence the title of the book—Curtis enters into a steamy affair with the detective. On the morning after their first night together, Anne Curtis wakes Rosen up in exactly the same manner Kira did me. Curtis speaks the same words Kira spoke. No wonder the scene was familiar to me. I wrote it.

"You're better than Anne Curtis," I said, pulling Kira onto my chest.

"Thank you," she whispered. "That scene between Wyatt and Anne is the most erotic thing I have ever read. It's ironic, when Zak bought me your book, I avoided reading it at first."

"Not much of a detective fiction fan, huh?"

"No. And I didn't want to hurt Zak's feelings anymore than I already had."

"What hap—"

"Let's not talk about it," she cut me off. "I've wanted to meet you for a long time, but I never thought I could be with you."

"Dream big, that's what I say." I laughed.

She punched my arm playfully and slid her hair down my chest, down my belly. "As I recall, Anne couldn't get enough of Wyatt," Kira said as she put me in her mouth.

Anne Curtis, of course, was lying about that. But for some odd reason I chose not to remind Kira of that.

Thread Hunting

We showered together. Kira was more playful in the light. I
wanted to take her to breakfast, but she turned me down. She
had acted out a dream. Dreams end in the morning, she said,
don't push them. To push them is to destroy them. We had
real lives to get back to. She had to go to her room and find
her paper on twentieth-century existential novels. I had to
find Zak.

We talked while she dressed. I asked about her loneliness. She didn't run away from the subject. She had been
born in Tokyo, but her father, a V.P. for Japan Airlines, was
transferred to Chicago when she was only four, to San
Francisco when she was nine, to L.A. when she was eleven,
and finally to New York when she was fourteen.

"I was kind of an army brat," she said sadly, "but without the support of others with the same fate. At least army
brats have the base. Then, when I was seventeen, my father
was given his big promotion and called back home."

"You stayed?"

"What choice did I have, really? I wasn't Japanese. I
wasn't American. I was both and neither. I had no good
friends here, but I had none there. My family in Japan were
strangers to me. In America at least, there is room for mis-
fits. At home—listen to me—sorry. In Japan, a misfit is
treated like a protruding nail. It is hammered down. I will not
be hammered down."

"I can see that. You're pretty brave," I said.

"No, Dylan. Only people with choices can be brave."

I asked again, as I had the night before, if she knew any
other of Zak's friends who might be able to help. The answer
was unchanged. She and Zak guarded their friendship jealously. They did not mix in the other's circle. She asked if she
could check in with me. I said that was a silly question. I
asked if we might dream again. She said we would have to
see what the night would bring. We left it there.

I went down to the local pancake house and had a breakfast that would have made my Uncle Saul jealous. Uncle
Saul was the only man I knew who could have lunch while

46

still eating breakfast. He had also consumed enough scotch whiskey to float an aircraft carrier. It worked for him. Saul was eighty-four and looked like sixty. Who needed bran and mineral water?

Somewhere between the cheese omelet and the corned beef hash, I managed to read the local paper. It was pretty much what you'd expect: two pages of local news, two pages of national and international news off the wire, an editorial about zoning variances, and twenty-three pages of advertisements.

I was about to put the paper down, when I overheard two guys who seemed to be groundskeepers from the college angrily discussing somebody named Jones. Their anger had a nasty racial bent. "Crack-pushin' nigger" topped the list of their favorite phrases. "Black bitch is just like her daddy" was a close second. I turned back to page three of the *Riversborough Gazette*. The headline read: "JONES JURY SELECTION TODAY."

Valencia Jones was big news in Riversborough. A freshman last year, Ms. Jones was stopped for a broken taillight as she was leaving town at Spring break. In spite of the fact that both her license and registration were in order, the cops searched her vehicle. In Riversborough, apparently, black face plus BMW equals reasonable cause. Their search netted two vials of a drug the cops were calling Isotope. Relatively cheap and easily produced, Isotope was a far more potent chemical variant of LSD. The paper said that the cops said that one of the vials found in the spare tire compartment of Ms. Jones' car contained enough Isotope to dose all of New York City. But since you can never believe what you read or what cops say about drugs, I figured there was enough Isotope in the vial to dose the Bronx. Anyway you cut it, that's a lot of stoned New Yorkers.

But beyond the drugs, the validity of the search, and the inherent racial baggage, there was Valencia Jones herself. As the paper pointed out in at least three instances, Valencia Jones was the daughter of the late Raman "Iceman" Jones. Until someone introduced him to the business end of a 9mm, the Iceman had controlled the heroin traffic between Stamford and Hartford, Connecticut. So, despite her exemplary scholastic record, her oft-stated desire to distance herself from her father's heinous life, and vows of innocence, no one seemed inclined to believe her. Her mother had even encountered difficulty finding a lawyer to take the case. No doubt my friend Larry Feld was previously committed to defending Jack the Ripper's latest devotee. Lord knows, this wasn't Jeffrey's kind of case.

Remembering I had to call both of them, I put the paper down. I felt sorry for Valencia Jones. I don't know why, exactly. I just did. But I had troubles of my own. However, as a gesture to racial harmony, I did a pratfall and dropped my tray of dirty dishes all over the two groundskeepers at the next table.

"Sorry," I said, "but this Jones trial's got me all riled up."

Zak's teachers were all pleasant. Uninformative, but pleasant. I got the usual stuff about how Zak and I looked alike and sounded alike. Zak was a good student, wrote a vicious term paper, didn't respond well to authority. None of them knew where he could have gotten to and they all missed his presence in class. His current English instructor, Professor Pewter, was all fired up about having read my novels. Overwritten, he thought, though he did rather enjoy the naughty bits. It was nice to know that my pornographic appeal crossed gender lines. It was nearly 1:00 P.M. when I headed back to my room to make some calls.

"So," MacClough began, "anything?"

"Depends."

"Depends on what?" He sounded down.

"Nothing on Zak unless we're interested in glowing testimonials," I said.

"What else?"

"What else can wait until this thing with Zak is resolved," I said.

"That Japanese chick, huh?" He perked up a bit.

"Something like that. What's wrong with you?"

"The safe-deposit box was a dead end as far as we're concerned."

"Empty," I asked, "or full of savings bonds?"

"Neither. Just some newspaper clippings about a drug bust upstate."

The hair stood up on the back of my neck. I was too stunned to speak.

"Klein!" MacClough shouted. "Klein, you still there?"

"This drug case recent?" I asked.

"I think so, but Fazio didn't exactly invite me along as a witness, you know? I got my info through Hurley."

"Did she give anything specific about the case, a name, maybe?"

"Yeah. Wait, I got it written down here somewhere." I heard him shuffling papers. "Here we are. Valen—"

"—cia Jones."

"Holy shit!"

"You know what I think, John?

"What?"

"I think we just found ourselves a place to start."

I filled him in on the little I knew of the case. He already knew of Raman "Iceman" Jones. MacClough had worked a tri-state narcotics task force and Raman Jones was one of the key targets of the investigation. Maybe we were just hungry for leads, but we both agreed that the timing of Zak's disappearance, Caliparri's murder, and the start of the trial were too close together to be coincidental. Now we had to go find a thread that tied them all together. MacClough said he'd come up my way as soon as he could, but in the meantime he'd go thread hunting in Castle-on-Hudson. When I asked him if he wanted me to tell Jeff about our theory, Johnny said no one was going to tell Jeff anything just yet.

"Your big brother strikes me as the kinda guy that likes to stick his nose into things whether his nose belongs there or not," MacClough explained. "Let's find something first."

"Agreed."

I hung up and punched in Larry Feld's office number. I didn't want to give myself any time to work out the permutations of an equation that involved my nephew, a drug kingpin's daughter, and a murdered cop. As I waited on the line, I distracted myself with fresh memories of Kira Wantanabe. Now there, I thought, there was someone with whom I'd be willing to work out any number of permutations.

Larry Feld was in court, but his secretary said that he had

left some material behind for me to read. I gave her the hotel's fax number and asked her to thank Larry for me. She said she would, but that when I got the fax I'd want to speak to Larry myself. There were things he needed to explain. That was Larry Feld's philosophy: everything needs explaining. Nothing is ever what it seems. He would even say: "My clients don't pay for me. They pay for my explanations." I couldn't wait.

Captain Acid

All the goodwill I'd built up with Zak's instructors in the morning had vanished with the passing of noon. The willing, smiling faces that had greeted me so eagerly earlier in the day grew sour and uneasy at the mention of Valencia Jones. Even Professor Pewter, my critic and fan, had lost his enthusiasm for my company. Some of the staff denied that anything had changed. They were just busier now. Some denied knowing who Valencia Jones was. The honest ones told me they had been warned not to discuss the case.

"Look, Mr. Klein," one of them said, "this isn't the real world. Our professional fates are decided in star chambers. We spend more time trying to learn whose asses to kiss and how to kiss them than on getting published. We are at the mercy of our chairman, the Dean, the Provost. Christ, it's positively feudal. When we've been warned off, it's not something to be taken lightly."

"My fucking nephew's missing."

"I'd like to help," he said, "but I don't know anything."

"I could just get the roster of the class Zak was in and find out if he and this Valencia Jones knew each other."

"Please, Mr. Klein, get the roster. You have my best wishes. Then it will be the administration's headache, not mine."

"Thanks." I patted him a bit too hard on the back. "I hope you get Social Security before you get tenure, you chickenshit son of a bitch. Have a nice day."

I figured I'd have a go with Zak's hallmates before trying to tackle the administration. I was sure they'd be more forthcoming. I was wrong. Kitty Genovese got more help from her neighbors. At least two people on Zak's hall slammed their doors in my face before I got to the last syllable of Valencia Jones' name. The third wise-guy who tried that routine, the kid in the room next door to Zak's, wasn't quick enough on the draw. I thought he was going to soil his pants when I pushed my way in.

"I'll call campus security!" he squealed, groping around his bookbag to produce a can of pepper spray. "I'll use this. I will!"

"Take it easy," I said, noticing his walls featured posters of Rush Limbaugh and Senator Joe McCarthy. "You got a thing for balding, fat, white men?"

The kid had no sense of humor and actually sprayed, but he was so nervous that the stream missed me. I slapped the can out of his hand before he got a second chance. I choked on some of the ambient mist and with my eyes beginning to tear, I just left. What good would it have done, anyway, I thought, to try and reason with an eighteen-year-old whose politics were just to the right of Vlad the Impaler. I washed my eyes out by a water fountain in the dorm lobby.

"Sir," a man's voice called to me, "slowly put your hands behind your head, kneel to the ground, and lie down on your belly."

"That little asshole!" I whispered out loud.

"Now!" the voice demanded.

"Yes, officer." I didn't need second sight to know there was a 9mm or a .38 pointed my way. As soon as my cheek touched the cold tile floor, strong hands locked my wrists in handcuffs behind my back. Those hands stood me up and pushed me forward.

"You have the right to remain silent—" he began.

"Actually," I corrected, "that's not true. I have the right not to incriminate myself. It's splitting hairs, but . . ."

He shoved me a little harder. MacClough had warned me never to get sarcastic with cops. It was guaranteed to piss them off. He was right, of course, but there are some times when it's hard to pass up a good straight line.

"You have the right to legal representation," he droned on. "If you cannot afford a lawyer, the court will provide one at no expense. Do you understand these rights?"

"*Je ne parle pas Anglais,*" I gave him Boyer with a faint hint of Chevalier.

Suddenly, I was eating dirty snow.

"Funny," the cop said, "how handcuffs can make a man lose his balance."

MacClough never said a word about speaking French. This too, it seemed, went unappreciated by law enforcement officials.

*　　　*　　　*

The holding cell at the Riversborough Station wasn't exactly the Tombs or Riker's Island, but it wasn't a suite at the Waldorf either. It was very Bauhaus, but I'm not sure what that school had to say about the delightful fragrance of old urine. I did not want for company there in the cage. Some guy in his twenties was sitting in the corner, waving his hand in front of his face as he stared at the light through splayed fingers. I figured he was autistic or tripping or both. I realized he was tripping out when he screamed: "Duck! Incoming red tracer, man."

Playing along, I hit the floor. "Thanks, dude. Isotope?" I asked, not expecting an answer.

"Awesome stuff, brother. Awesome."

Before I could ask a follow-up, he started with the hand waving again. I relaxed. I knew my cagemate would warn me about incoming red tracers.

"Okay," a fat cop said, putting his key in the door, "which one of you is the French Legionnaire?"

"*C'est moi!*" I jumped to attention and saluted.

"You're out of here, Beau Geste."

"But I didn't make my call," I protested.

"You picked up English fast. Listen, wiseass, there's two guards from campus security waiting outside with a car to escort you to a meeting."

"I don't have any meeting."

"You do if you wanna get out of here." He smiled. "Or maybe you'd like to stay and keep Captain Acid here company."

I looked over at the corner and turned to my jailer. "Let's get to that meeting. I mustn't keep my fans waiting."

The security guards were typical square-badgers, cop wannabes with chips on their shoulders. They pretty much ignored me, especially when I had the nerve to ask where we were going. When I mentioned Valencia Jones, however, they suggested that I relax and shut up or go back to jail. I went with the first option.

We parked by the school's power station and took a nice tour of the campus' network of underground tunnels. I was

53

glad my escorts knew where they were headed, because I sure as hell didn't. Once we got into the maze, one tunnel looked like the next. I asked my chaperons why there weren't any signs to mark the way. I was told that stealing the signposts was a traditional part of hazing for all the frats and sororities. The signs went up during the last week of August. By the end of the first week of September, they were gone. I could tell my two square-badges just hated the type of students who would take those signs. They much preferred the assholes with pepper spray.

When we finally came up from the depths, we landed in a large reception area. Raised walnut panels covered the walls and portraits of unsmiling men covered the panels. There were several green leather settees arranged about the room. I was delivered to a silver-haired woman seated behind an ornate oaken desk stained to match the walls. She was a handsome woman on the wrong side of fifty-five. She had a pleasant smile, but something in the lines of her face told me she was not to be trifled with.

"Thank you, gentlemen," she dismissed my escorts. "We can handle Mr. Klein from here. Can't we, Mr. Klein?

"Absolutely."

The security guards disappeared back into the tunnels.

"Have a seat, Mr. Klein. Dean Dallenbach will be with you shortly. Can I get you a cup of coffee or tea while you wait?"

"Coffee, thanks. Milk, no sugar."

A buzzer sounded on her desk. "You can go in, sir. The Dean is ready for you. I'll serve your coffee inside with Dean Dallenbach's tea."

Dallenbach was younger than I'd expected, fifty maybe. He was suspiciously corporate looking right down to his wing tips. His blue Brooks Brothers three-piece was smartly tailored, no unseemly bulges along his long, svelte figure. He was Burt Lancaster without the perfect smile.

"Have a seat, Mr. Klein," he offered. There were no sharp edges in his voice. "You've been making quite a nuisance of yourself, haven't you: striking Prof. Zanter and accosting a student named . . . Robert Birch?"

"John Birch was more like it."

"We don't screen for politics here, Mr. Klein."

The secretary served our drinks with tea cakes and cucumber sandwiches cut into wedges, their crusts trimmed to perfection. I ate and drank while he gave me a lecture about proper decorum and campus policy. His tone was friendly enough and his flecked green eyes sparkled with pride as he went over a brief history of the school and the accomplishments of its alumni.

"I'm sold," I said, finishing my last sandwich. "I'll come back and get my degree."

He looked horrified.

"Only joking," I winked.

He seemed relieved. "Back to the issue at hand. What have you to say about your earlier actions concerning Prof. Zanter and Mr. Birch?"

"Not much," I confessed. "Maybe Prof. Zanter misinterpreted a strong pat on the back."

"Possibly your calling him, and I quote: 'A chicken-shit son of a bitch,' led him to misconstrue your meaning. Do you think?"

"I guess I can see that now," I said.

"And as for your assault on Mr. Birch?"

"The little weasel pepper-sprayed me without provocation."

"Pardon my skepticism, Mr. Klein, but breaking into a student's room is certainly provocation enough."

"Is that what I did?"

He stood up from behind his desk. "See here, Mr. Klein, I can appreciate your situation. I know about your nephew. I too am gravely concerned for Zak's safety. I am only too willing to cooperate with you and or your brother in your efforts to discover your nephew's whereabouts. But I cannot allow you to turn this institution on its ear in the process. I will tolerate no further use of threat or strong-arm tactics aimed at the faculty, students, staff, or administration. Is that understood?"

"It is," I answered humbly. "And I'm sorry for any trouble I might've caused."

"We understand, Mr. Klein."

"Could you tell me," I wondered, "if my nephew and Valencia Jones were ever in the same class?"

For the first time since my arrival in his office, Dallenbach's face went cold. Then, as he fiddled with his computer keyboard, his expression went from cold to outright angry.

"No, sir, they never shared a class." He swung his monitor around to show me.

"Thanks. Why is everyone around here so sensitive about Valencia Jones?"

"Riversborough College is neither Harvard nor Berkeley nor is it Brooklyn College," he sniped at me. "We are privately funded and have a small but secure endowment. We cannot afford much scandal. Through vigilance and good fortune, we have been able to keep Riversborough out of the drug culture loop."

"Until now."

"Yes, Mr. Klein, until now. And we do not plan on having a repeat of this ugliness anytime soon. We guard Riversborough's reputation jealously. I make no apologies for that."

"I can appreciate that," I empathized, "but you must realize that if there's someone producing Isotope in town—"

"Stop there. I don't accept your premise. This was an isolated incident."

"You better rethink your position on that. I was just in a holding cell with some kid tripping out of his mind."

That gave Dean Dallenbach pause. I could see him trying to formulate a reasonable response, but, "I'll look into it," was all he said on the subject.

"You should."

"You may go now, Mr. Klein. I've seen to it that no charges will be leveled against you. I am afraid, however, that I must ask you to route any of your investigations through these offices. If, in the future, you wish to deal with any member of the faculty or student body, you must seek written permission to do so. And if any person denies you access, that answer will be considered final and binding. There will be no appeal. Is that understood?" It wasn't a question, really, so I just nodded. "Excellent. Good day to you, sir, and much success in locating your nephew. The next time me meet, I hope it will be under more favorable circumstances."

I was being dismissed. Dallenbach had pretty much driven a stake into the heart of my investigation, but he did it with a smile. He'd warned me and he wanted it on record. I wasn't about to listen to him. Zak's life was more important than the school's prestige. But I would have to be a bit more restrained. From this point on, I knew someone would be watching.

You'll Be Wrong

The desk clerk grabbed me on the way up to my room at the Old Watermill and handed me a few sheets of fax paper. He reminded me that the inn was going to throw its weekly fish fry tonight. I thanked him, but told him I'd have to take a pass on the fried fish. Before parting company, I asked him to deliver two cups of coffee to the campus security officers parked across the street in the blue minivan. The clerk didn't bat an eye and wondered if I might not have a message to deliver with the coffee?

I said I did. "Tell them I know how bad surveillance duty sucks. Tell them if they should feel nature call, to just piss into the empty cups."

It was a real Hollywood gesture, but having been there recently, I figured I was excused. The clerk loved it. I didn't imagine he got to do a whole lot of Hollywood material there in the land of fish fries. I slipped him a twenty for the coffee and future considerations. It was, after all, Jeffrey's money.

I tossed the fax on the bed and headed straight for the shower. The jail stink came off in layers. As I washed, I went over my little conference with Dean Dallenbach. He'd been relatively civil and more understanding than I had reason to expect, but, in spite of my brave front, I was a bit unnerved by my visit to city jail and the dean's office. I don't know, maybe it was the town getting to me. I was beginning to think Riversborough was the kind of place that was best experienced on a picture postcard. There were probably lots of nasty things buried beneath the snow.

Larry's cover letter read like this:

Klein—

Schmuck! It was the Boatswain case, not Hernandez.

If you said that up front, I could've had this shit for you almost immediately. Read between the lines and between the lines you can't see. As you're reading, think about why people you're close to refer to this using Hernandez's name. When you reach a con-

58

clusion, you'll be wrong. Call me for the truth.

You owe me, baby,

Feld

Oh that Larry, he was such a charmer. Even when he did right, he made you want to poke his eyes out. And when Larry mentioned reading between the lines, he wasn't kidding. Pages two and three of the fax were simply compilations of headlines from the three New York City dailies. Atop page two, there was a handwritten message from Feld advising me that the headlines first appeared in the papers between March 14, 1972 and January 4, 1973 and that they appeared in chronological order. This is what I looked at:

March 14, 1972—
Post **BOY-NAPPED**   *News* **RIVERDALE TEEN TAKEN**
Times **CARDIOLOGIST'S SON TAKEN**

March 16, 1972—
Post **RING FINGER, RANSOM NOTE**
News **RANSOM IN RIVERDALE**
Times **MACABRE NOTE RECEIVED**

March 19, 1972—
Post **FEDS BLOW IT**   *News* **DELIVERY DISASTER**
Times **CAPTURE ATTEMPT GOES AWRY**

March 22, 1972—
Post **NEW FINGER, NEW DEMANDS**
News **GRISLY DO-OVER**   *Times* **NEW DEMANDS**

March 23, 1972—
Post **SPOOKED**   *News* **NAPPERS-NO SHOW**
Times **KIDNAPPERS REFUSE RANSOM**

March 28, 1972—
Post **HOPES FADE**   *News* **GOING, GOING . . .**

Times **FEDERAL AGENTS PESSIMISTIC**

April 22, 1972—
Post **HERO COP FINDS BODY**
News **...GONE, BOY'S BODY FOUND** *Times* **TRAGIC ENDING**

April 23, 1972—
*Post***COWARD'S WAY OUT—KIDNAPPER EATS BULLET**
News **KIDNAPPER SUICIDE ONLY FITTING**
Times **ALLEGED KIDNAPPER FOUND DEAD**

April 28, 1972—
Post **KIDNAP BOY BURIED—HERO COP PROMOTED**
News **BOATSWAIN BOY LAID TO REST TODAY**
Times **BOATSWAIN BURIAL TODAY**

June 30, 1972—
Post **HERO COP UNDER GUN**
News **POLICE TO PROBE CRUSADING COP**
*Times***INVESTIGATION IN BOATSWAIN KIDNAPPING**

October 12, 1972—
Post **FAMILY AFFAIR—KIDNAPPER'S BROTHER FOR MACHETE KILLING**
News **HERNANDEZ BROTHER UP FOR MURDER ONE**

January 4, 1973—
Post **HERO COP CLEARED** *News* **MACCLOUGH IS CLEAN**
Times **BOATSWAIN CASE CLOSED**

The final page of the fax was a grainy photostat of a redacted NYPD document dated May 7, 1972. It was a formal complaint and request for investigation sent to the Internal Affairs Division of the NYPD located on Poplar Street in Brooklyn. The name of the officer requesting the investigation was blacked out as were all the names on the document. But one thing was clear, one police officer was accusing another of executing a suspect in a high-profile case. Given the date of the complaint and the headlines on the previous pages, filling in the redacted names became rather easy guesswork. Fazio had made the complaint against MacClough.

I was pretty sure I now had a grasp on everyone's attachment to the Hernandez or Boatswain or whatever-you-wanted-to-call-it case. MacClough would never consider himself a hero for doing his job. Furthermore, John would consider himself a failure for getting to the boy too late. And even though he'd been cleared of wrongdoing, MacClough would see the investigation as a black mark, a scar on his reputation. I don't think this was the type of thing he would discuss with anyone. As for my eternally pragmatic brother, his motivation for involving MacClough was apparent. If MacClough had been willing to risk so much for the Boatswain boy, a boy he had no obvious emotional ties to, then imagine what MacClough might do when trying to locate his best friend's nephew. Jeffrey also knew that MacClough would look at this as a second chance. This time he might get to the boy before it was too late. The reason for the tension between Fazio and MacClough was palpable, and now, completely understandable.

So why was it, if I had such a strong grasp on all the players' motivations, that I felt so uneasy? Because I couldn't get Larry's caveat out of my head: "When you reach a conclusion, you'll be wrong." Of course, if Larry had bothered to forward the actual newspaper articles along with the headlines, I might have felt a bit more secure in my analysis. But that wasn't the way Larry operated. He needed to be needed. It's why he did favors for me at all. It was sort of a dance we did that went back to when we were kids.

As I picked up the phone to do my part of the cha-cha there was a knock at the door. I put the phone back in its cradle and answered the door: "Who's there?"

"I have come to show you what the night has brought." Kira stepped shyly into my room. "I didn't want to come."

"Why did you?"

"My heart gave me no choice."

Ice Fishing

I hate this part of me, the part that could stand back and rub its white-gloved fingers along the edges of perfection look-ing for hidden dust. I don't know if I was born with it or if it is the Brooklyn in me, but my nature runs towards distrust. Well, that's not exactly true. To be precise, I more readily accept the wrong, the failed, the negative numbers. It isn't affection, but comfort. It is easier to believe deformity.

I was hating myself a lot right then, Kira sleeping softly beside me. She had come to me in spite of herself, kissed me until I lost all sense of time and place. She stunned me with the eloquence of her surrender. And there I was—my lips and beard wet with her, her scent filling every corner of the night—unable to sleep as I looked for the fault lines along the gentle curves of her torso. And what wrong had she done other than to like me and my silly books, to enjoy the feel of me inside her?

I thought back to the previous night, my pulp detective suspiciously poking through the woman's handbag with the barrel of his gun. Wasn't that what I was doing now, sorting through Kira's every nuance: the way she threw back her head when I licked her breast, her every sigh and shudder?

Wasn't I as cheap and hollow as my own detective, searching for duplicity not in a handbag, but where shadows fell across the breathing landscape of my lover's body? No, I was worse.

"Ummm." Kira rolled over in my arms, stretching. "You're still up?"

"Yeah."

"Is anything the matter?"

"Nothing," I lied.

"Uncle Dylan is a bad liar." She ran her finger over my mouth. "Lies are transparent in the dark."

She replaced her finger with her lips and rolled me over onto my back. Even as she kissed me into forgetfulness, I fought a quiet battle with my own suspicions. Suspicions which said much more about me than their target.

Kira was up already when I opened my eyes. She was dressed and seated on the edge of the bed reading my fax. When she noticed I was awake, she smiled, putting the papers down on the desk.

"Come on," she said, "I want to take you to breakfast."

"What about class?"

"I'm a diligent student, but even I give myself a rest on Saturday."

I showered. Before we headed downstairs, I let her in on my new found life of crime and my run-in with Dean Dallenbach. I told her we were going to be followed and that I would understand if she didn't want to be seen with me. She could, she said, handle Dean Dallenbach's wrath, but that if she didn't get some food in her soon, I'd have a corpse on my hands.

"Forget that," I said. "The hotel charges extra for heavy-duty cleanup."

My pal was back at work behind the front desk. When I stopped to ask him how the coffee delivery went, he was inexplicably cool to me. He barely managed an; "Okay," before turning his back on me. I figured it had to be my morning breath or Kira's presence at my side. And since I'd brushed and gargled, I supposed it was Kira. I was really beginning to hate this town. When I opened my mouth to call the desk clerk on his attitude, Kira tugged me by the elbow and urged me out the door.

"What an asshole!" I hissed as we walked out into a snow shower. "What was it, you think; the difference in our ages or your being Japanese?"

"Neither." She winked. "I don't think he likes Jews."

"That's it!"

I chased her down the street and threw her into a snow-drift. With a lusty smile, she beckoned me closer. When I brought my face nearer to hers, she rubbed a handful of snow in my mouth. I kissed her anyway, but as I came up for air, I noticed a blue minivan parked not twenty feet away at the curb. I had no appetite for performance. I picked her up and we went on to breakfast.

63

"I don't mean to pry," she said, squirming in her seat, "but did that fax on your desk have anything to do with Zak?"

"No, not directly. It's just some research I'm doing for my next book," I lied for no good reason. I was better at it in daylight. "And you're not prying. I'm glad someone in this goddamned place is genuinely interested in Zak."

"Any word on him?"

I waved to the waitress for more coffee. "No, but I think there's a connection between Zak's disappearance and the Valencia Jones trial."

"What makes you think that?"

I hesitated until the waitress had refilled our cups and gone. I told Kira about Detective Caliparri's murder and the newspaper clippings in his deposit box.

"So there's no direct link?" She asked the obvious question.

"None so far, but I haven't had a chance to establish one. And now with Dean Dallenbach's restrictions . . ." I looked out the front window at my shadows in the minivan. "Do you know if my nephew and Valencia Jones were acquainted?"

"I'm sorry, I don't."

"Don't sweat it. It's just a hunch anyway. But the fact that everyone in Riversborough is so uptight about Valencia Jones, makes me think I've got something."

"Maybe you do." She tried to sound encouraging, but the turned-down corners of her mouth betrayed her.

"If there's a connection, I'll find it in spite of this town."

We finished our breakfasts in relative silence. But our waitress was the type of person who couldn't stand silence and decided to strike up a conversation.

"Terrible thing about that boy up at Cyclone Ridge, eh?"

"What's Cyclone Ridge?" I wondered.

"A ski resort just north of town," Kira said.

"Well anyhow," the waitress plowed on, "this boy gets tanked real good at the bar and goes solo night skiing on Twister Run. That's the steepest trail they got up there, honey," she wanted me to know.

"Did he get hurt badly?" Kira asked.

"No, honey, he got dead. Neck was broken in three places, but the pine tree was barely scratched." The waitress chuckled. "Here's your check. And don't forget to have a nice day."

"I guess you're not going to want to go skiing now," Kira feigned disappointment.

"Ski! Jewish boys from Brooklyn don't ski. The closest thing we had to mountains were the road bumps on Flatlands Avenue. And they paved those over when I was eight. Anyway, I've got a few errands to run."

"I'll come with you."

"These kinds of things are better done alone," I said, leaning to kiss her cheek. "Don't hate me."

"I couldn't."

"Tonight?"

"We'll see," she said. "We'll see."

She snapped up the bill and was gone. I watched out the window to see if the boys in the minivan were interested in Kira. Nope, they didn't move. They only had eyes for me.

*   *   *

The cop at the front desk was doing the crossword puzzle. I didn't recognize him from either of my previous two trips to the Riversborough Station and if he recognized me, he wasn't letting on. When he got around to asking me what I wanted, I said I'd like to visit one of the prisoners.

"Sorry," he said, "fresh out."

He went on to say that they hadn't had a prisoner for two weeks. He was unimpressed when I explained that I had been a prisoner just the day before.

"Who brought you in?" he asked.

"Campus security."

"Were you officially charged?"

"No."

"Then," the cop said, "you don't count, do you?"

I told him it was up to him as to whether I counted or not, but at the moment, I wasn't interested in me. There was

65

another guy in the holding cage, I explained, and he was trip-ping out somewhere beyond the moons of Saturn. Grudgingly, the cop punched in a few keys on the computer.

"Prisoner's name?"

I said I didn't know. That went over like termites at a toothpick convention.

"Look, mister, you better stop wasting my time or you sure as hell will be a prisoner in this jail."

Disregarding his own words, the desk cop continued punching at his keyboard. I guess before he got really mad at me, he wanted to make sure I was wrong. He turned his monitor around so I could see it. He brought up two weeks worth of booking sheets and arrests. Only one screen had a name on it. That name was mine. And in bold letters beneath my name, it read:

"RELEASED TO DEAN DALLENCBACH. NO CHARGES TO BE FILED"

"But I'm telling you," I pushed my luck, "there was another guy in the cell with me: blond, long hair, earring, twenty, maybe twenty-one."

"Well, I wasn't here yesterday and this screen's the only thing I got to go by."

When I asked to see the fat cop who was on duty when I was being held, the guy at the desk answered: "No can do. Sergeant Wick left last night for an ice-fishing tournament up in northern Ontario."

The other cops I had met when I'd first come into town were similarly indisposed. How convenient, I thought, for everybody but me. All I had wanted to do was to ask my cagemate where he'd gotten hold of his Isotope. Now, it seemed, I was the one who was hallucinating. Unfortunately, it was a wee bit late in the game for me to be having flash-backs. I was getting jerked around something fierce. But there was an upside to getting jerked around. It meant there were people in Riversborough with things to hide. Maybe one of those things was my nephew. It was time for me to get MacClough up here.

"Thank you, officer."

66

"That's it?" he sounded sad to see me go.

"See that flat spot?" I pointed to my forehead. "I got that from pounding my head into the wall. I've learned when to stop."

*　　　　*　　　　*

Now that Kira wasn't with me, I was prepared to tear into the desk clerk at the Old Watermill. He wasn't in. Probably gone ice fishing. I picked up my messages. MacClough and Jeff had called. Neither one requested an urgent callback. I swiped a copy of the local paper from the lounge and went up to my room to catch a few hours of real sleep. Passion is great, but it does tend to get in the way of normal sleeping patterns.

I stretched out on the big down comforter and began wading through the local paper. I got as far as the picture on page three. It was an enlargement of the driver's license photo of the skier killed at Cyclone Ridge. His name was Steven Markum, an unemployed chair-lift mechanic from Plattsburgh, New York. But I knew him better as Captain Acid.

A Certain Romance

MacClough agreed to come. He thought I was making progress. If getting someone killed was making progress, then he was right. It didn't feel like progress to me. It was difficult to discern what it felt like with a six-pack and half a bottle of vodka in me. I wasn't any good at regulating hurt with alcohol. I don't think anybody is, really. But there are people, people like MacClough and my Uncle Saul, who derived a certain liquid catharsis from binging. Even in the nausea of the next day, they found a strange satisfaction which escaped me, a certain romance. It wasn't romance I was looking for.

I could not remove my gaze from the newspaper, from Steven Markum's impassive face. I thanked God, for lack of a reasonable alternative that it wasn't one of those photographs with penetrating eyes. They were neither the eyes of the omniscient oculist nor eyes to pin you wriggling to the wall. They were eyes bored of waiting on line at the motor vehicles office. I raised my glass to Steven Markum. We were quite a pair, Markum and me, numb and number. Numbness was underrated.

"To Captain Acid! Beware of incoming red tracers."

He remained unmoved.

There was knocking at my door. I made myself not hear it and continued on the second half of the bottle. It would not go down so easily as the first. The headache had since started crawling into my sinuses and dinner wasn't liking it too much in my stomach. The knocking grew louder, insistent.

"Dylan!" Kira's voice was worried. "Dylan, are you all right?"

I did not answer.

"Dylan, please let me in."

Again, I did not answer.

"Dylan! Please. I hear you. What's wrong?"

"You're wrong!" I lashed out. "Get the fuck outta here!"

"Dylan!"

"Play time is over, Kira. Go and find some other kids and

play grown-up with them." I could be so brave behind a closed door.

"I'm frightened, Dylan."

"For chrissakes," I blustered, "stop calling me Dylan. I know my fucking name!"

"Do you want me to get some help?"

"No! I want you to go fuck somebody your own age and leave me the fuck alone. I don't want you here."

"Dylan—"

"Shut up!" I paused. "You know what I've been wondering, Kira?"

"No, I don't."

"I've been wondering how you got so good at fucking old men. I—"

"Don't do this, Dylan, please."

"I'll do what I want. Answer the question."

"Please, Dylan, don't—"

"Answer the fucking question!"

"What did I do wrong?" she quivered. "Why do you want to hurt me like this?"

"I'm not hurting you. I'm doing you a favor. Now do me one and get the fuck away from me!"

There was silence. No more pleading. No footsteps. No sobbing. Then:

"I hate you. I hate you for this!"

That made two of us. If she hesitated for a moment or ran down the hall, I couldn't say. I was far too busy gagging on my own self-pity to notice.

Guilt

I watched MacClough stroll out of the gate, carry-on bag in hand. And once again I was dismayed by his looks. It wasn't that I'd forgotten how fatigued and bloated he appeared at my Dad's funeral, but getting to the root of his sudden weight gain wasn't exactly at the top of my punch list. Extra bulk or not, he was still a pro and followed my instructions to the letter. He did not look for me in the crowd, though he knew I was there watching. He confirmed his car rental and headed for the phone bank just to the right of the Riversborough Chamber of Commerce sign. I watched him slowly punch in a number as he read it off a slip of paper. About seventy-five feet away, on the other side of the terminal, another phone rang. I picked up.

"You watched too many Hitchcock movies when you were a kid," he said. "Are you sure this cloak-and-dagger crap is necessary in such a cockamamy little town? Jesus, Klein, the Sheepshead Bay Diner is bigger than this airport."

"And it has better cheesecake, but you could barely land a helicopter in the parking lot. Trust me, John, these precautions are necessary. Like I told you on the phone last night, I've had these two clowns on my ass for days. I'm sure I lost them on the way here, but I can't be certain they're not bearding for someone I haven't spotted. Did you make a reservation at the Old Watermill Inn?"

"I did."

"Great. It's good to have you around," my voice smiled. "I've been tripping over my dick in the dark around here."

"I bet that's not the only thing you've been doing with it."

I ignored that. "My room in an hour."

"Klein!"

"Yeah."

"I'll stay on the line after you hang up. If anybody follows you besides the two guys you know about, I'll spot 'em."

"Thanks."

I took a detour back to the hotel that led me past Cyclone

70

Ridge. The chairlifts were pretty much idle and I could only spot a few lonely souls working their way down the ski trails. That was no surprise. Death on the slopes isn't much of a selling point. With time, though, people would forget. The papers would move onto another story. People would return. Accidents will happen. But so will murder. And murder is what happened here. I could feel it in the marrow of my bones. I also felt responsible. For although I might never be able to prove it, I knew as surely as the sun burned in the sky, that if Steven Markum had never met me, he would be alive today. I wasn't nearly as confident that I knew how to live with that kind of guilt. It was a long ride back down the mountain.

I didn't even look to see who was behind the desk when I got back to the Old Watermill. I went straight up to my room. As I stepped in, a strong hand grabbed my collar and pulled me to the ground. I had a mouthful of carpet and one armed pinned painfully against my back. Something round and very cold was jabbed into the soft spot behind my ear. Then, in one eternal instant, I heard the door lock snap shut and the metallic click of a gun hammer striking.

I was lifted up, not by God's right hand, but by MacClough's.

"Asshole!" He shook me. "You're not paying attention."

"I am now."

We hugged. He pushed me back to arm's length and stared through me. I could tell he didn't like the view.

"What's the matter with you?"

"Oh nothing, John." I pulled out of his grasp. "My Dad just died. My nephew's missing. I crapped out in Hollywood. I've managed to get pepper-sprayed, arrested, and get somebody killed. And last night, because I was too busy beating the shit out of myself to notice what I might be doing to anyone else, I ruined the most exciting relationship I've probably ever had. So no, John, nothing's wrong."

He lifted his pants leg and holstered his .38. "Stop feeling sorry for yourself or just go home. You're not gonna do anybody any good if you're gonna live inside your head. I can't watch your back and mine at the same time."

"Why not, you got eye troubles?" I wondered.

"My eyes are fine. It's just that there seems to be a lot of people interested in your flat Jewish ass. I don't know if I can keep track. Maybe we should just give out numbers like the deli counter at Waldbaums."

"I was followed?"

"You were," he confirmed. "The first guy looked like a surfer in a ski suit. You know the type, sunbleached blond, funky sunglasses, muscles from here to there. Didn't you spot him?"

"Half the population of Riversborough looks like that. The other half looks like the smartest kid in your third grade class, only bigger and with bad skin."

"The other guy was a Fed. I worked on task forces with a hundred guys just like him. From the way he dressed, he might as well have had FBI, ATF, or DEA printed on the back of his suit. The problem with those guys is, even though they're trained not to advertise who they are, they can't stand for the whole world not to know. One time I was on a surveillance and it was really late and we'd been in the car for hours. We'd told every joke, every bar story, every sex story we could think of. Finally, I turned to one of these FBI guys and ask him why he became a Fed. You know what he said to me?" MacClough started laughing.

"No."

"He says becoming a Special Agent is as close to being a superhero as he could get. What a fuckin' idiot, huh?"

"Good thing he liked Superman cartoons better than the Roadrunner."

We both laughed at that. Then it got very quiet.

"I love you, man." He hugged me again, but very tight, almost desperately. "I just want you to know that."

"I know that, John. I know."

"Good." He let me go. "Let's take a look inside the mini-bar. We got a lot to talk about before our trip tomorrow."

"Where're we going?"

"To jail."

"Been there. Done that."

"Not this jail," he said. "And don't worry, we're not staying. We're just visiting."

"One of your relatives?" I teased.

72

"No, shithead, Valencia Jones."

"How did—"

"Don't ask," MacClough ordered. "Don't ask."

And I didn't. John was halfway to the minibar when someone knocked on the door. It was Kira. My heart was in my throat. MacClough whispered for me to get rid of her. I got rid of him instead, sort of. He fit nicely into the closet.

When she stepped in, tears were running down her cheeks. I opened my mouth. Nothing came out. There are certain hurts for which an apology is an insult. I dropped to my knees and pressed the side of my face to her belly. She ran her fingers through what was left of my gray hair. She kissed the top of my head before dropping down to her knees. Once we kissed, we could not stop. And not for a second did I think of John Francis MacClough hiding there in my closet.

The Baby Jesus at Christmastime

She wouldn't let me explain about the night before. Kira understood about demons. Most of the time, she said, we speak for them. Sometimes they speak for us. And when she swore she didn't hate me, I nearly believed her.

She got curious about my leaving town for the day, but I deflected her questions. If MacClough hadn't been in the closet, I might have told Kira about our day trip to meet with Valencia Jones. But MacClough could be a security freak. As he didn't want me to tell my own brother details of what we were doing, I didn't figure he'd be happy with me telling Kira. I held her for a moment and sent her on her way.

Closing one door, I opened another.

"I admire you, John. It takes balls to come out of the closet so late in life."

"Start running!" He took out his .38. "I'll give you a five minute head start. It'll take me that long to get the feeling back in my legs."

"Stop complaining. I'm going to take a shower."

"The only thing I'm complaining about is that I couldn't watch. Next time," he winked, "I'm hiding behind the curtains. She sounds unbelievable, but you disappointed me, Klein. You didn't beg once or squeal like a pig."

"Fuck you."

"So," he wondered, putting away his pistol, "what was that all about?"

I handed MacClough the newspaper article about Steven Markum's death. I stood by for a second as he read through it.

"Mr. Vodka and I took it out on her. We didn't quite tear her heart out, but it wasn't for lack of effort." I stepped into the bathroom.

"Jews can't drink," he shouted through the door. "Don't you know that yet?"

"Try explaining that to my Uncle Saul."

"Coffee and sponge cake, that's how your people punish themselves. Besides, you didn't get this kid killed."

I turned the water on full blast to drown out

MacClough's voice. I wasn't ready to hear his "It wasn't your fault" lecture. Not yet.

*   *   *

I rolled over and looked at the clock. I cursed MacClough's birth and answered the phone. It was one of those automated voices reminding me it was time to get up. I told the voice to stick something up its mechanical ass, but it insisted upon repeating itself.

"Room 8, in accordance with your request, this is your 4:45 AM wake-up call. It has been our pleasure to serve you. Press the pound sign if you wish this call to be repeated in ten minutes. Room 8, in accordance..."

It might have been my request, but it was MacClough's idea. My only consolation was that John himself was already up, out, and on the road. I emptied my bladder, brushed my teeth, and struggled to get dressed. I threw on MacClough's ancient peacoat and a ski cap and left the Old Watermill via a side exit. I found his rented car parked at the curb. There was a road map on the front passenger seat. MacClough had marked in red a rest stop along the interstate. I checked my watch. I had an hour and a half to get there.

*   *   *

I was on my second cup of coffee when he walked up to my table.

"You look better in that coat than I do," I said. "Wanna trade?"

I had asked him that question in one form or another at least once a winter for the last ten years. He always said no. He had kept his peacoat for over three decades, since his discharge from the Navy. And like my motorcycle jacket, his peacoat represented something to him that wasn't easily explained. It was more than nostalgia or aesthetics. It was as if part of his being was stored in the coat itself. I don't know, it was sort of like how a kid feels about a baby blanket.

"Keep it," he answered. "Come on, we gotta go."

I nearly spit coffee through my nose.

75

The trial was being held in Mohawkskill, New York, a funky little town just across Lake Champlain from Burlington, Vermont. Mohawkskill, New York resembled the part of the state I grew up in about as much as Bobo Dioulasso resembled Beijing. One thing I noticed right away, there weren't many Mohawks in Mohawkskill. There weren't many Blacks or Asians or Latinos either. And for some odd reason, I got the feeling that there wasn't much of a push to place a menorah on the village green next to the baby Jesus at Christmastime. Go ahead, call me a cynic, but I was having some difficulty believing that a young African American woman, the daughter of a murdered drug kingpin, apprehended with a large quantity of hallucinogenic chemicals in her BMW, was going to find a jury of peers, let alone a sympathetic ear, in Mohawkskill.

"So," I spoke up, "how did our clothes and car swapping charade go?"

"Fine. I felt like I was in a conga line," he laughed. "They all followed your car like good little soldiers. Imagine their surprise when I pulled to the side of the road and took your coat off. I started stretching and turned right around so they could all get a good look at my face."

"They probably felt like they got caught jacking off in the bathroom by their mothers."

"Klein, you got a way with words."

We pulled into the county jail parking lot and headed·on upstairs. If the staff wasn't exactly friendly, they were, at least, cooperative. They seemed less emotionally invested in Valencia Jones' fate than the folks in Riversborough. But when we met the county prosecutor outside the visitors' area, I realized I was wrong. This guy was out for blood.

"Mr. MacClough, Mr. Klein, I'm A.D.A. Bob Smart," he said, shaking our hands without enthusiasm.

Bob Smart was a rotund little man with cruel eyes, thick lips, and a bad comb-over hairdo. He had pudgy, sweaty hands and a wardrobe that would have been tasteless in the '70s. He would have been easy to dismiss, but I had seen his type operate before. He practically begged you to underestimate him and, if you did, he'd eat you for lunch.

"Can I ask you gentlemen what this meeting is about?"

"Well, Mr. Smart," MacClough began, "it's—"

"Why," I wondered, cutting Johnny off, "isn't Miss Jones' attorney here?"

"I'm sure I don't know, Mr. Klein," Smart dropped his friendly voice. "You'll have to ask Miss Jones. Let me repeat my initial question."

"No need for that," MacClough turned on the charm, "we have no wish to interfere with your case. I have all the confidence in the world that you'll prove Miss Jones to be guilty as sin. We're here because Mr. Klein is researching a book on Miss Jones' late father, Raman Jones."

I improvised. "I'm going to call it *The Iceman Goeth.*"

"I like it," Smart approved. He nodded to the guard. "Go on in. You've got fifteen minutes." We did the handshake thing again. He mentioned that he'd look for my book on the shelves. We watched him waddle down the hall.

"You think he bought it?" I whispered.

"Not for a second, but he couldn't really stop us. And next time, let me do all the talking to the D.A. You almost blew it with that question about Jones', lawyer."

"How?"

"Later."

We were patted down and ushered into a drab room with barred windows. Everything, from the chairs to the ashtray on the table, was bolted and/or welded down. Valencia Jones was led into the room by a female guard through a thick metal door. She was pushed into her chair and her right leg was cuffed to the chair leg.

"There is to be no physical contact with the prisoner," the guard instructed. "I'll be right outside that door. If you need me, there's a call button under the table." She checked her watch. "Fifteen minutes and counting."

Valencia Jones wasn't beautiful nor was she as plain as her newspaper pictures. She was a medium girl: medium height, medium weight, medium. She had skin the color of dark coffee and sad, sad eyes. If I were facing ten to twenty-five years in a state prison, I, too, would have sad eyes. The rest of her face told no tales. Her expression remained blank until the guard was fully out of the room.

"You look like Zak," she smiled. Then, catching herself, went back into her shell.

She had answered my question without it even being asked.

"Your lawyer told you why we're here?" MacClough half asked, half stated.

"You the man?" Jones sneered at MacClough.

"Yeah, I used to be a cop. I used to chase your father around."

"Fuck my father!" Tears poured out of her. "Do you think if my father had been a dentist or a Yale professor that I would be here now, tethered to a chair like a wild animal? My father's the reason I'm here."

"Your father's not the one who got caught smuggling the felony weight drugs. You were."

"You know, Mr. MacClough, I spent my life trying to deny my blackness. But when you're in here, that's impossible. You told my lawyer that you were looking for Zak and that you might be able to help me. So far all I hear is that you sound like every other cop. You talk about my father and you think I'm guilty."

"You're not guilty?" I asked.

"No, sir," she said to me, "I am not. But if you're going to ask me how the drugs got in my car, I can't tell you. If you expect me to prove my innocence to you, I can't. All I know is that Zak believed in me enough to ask his father to represent me."

MacClough and I were dumbfounded. "Zak asked my brother to represent you?"

"He did, but Zak's dad gave him some nonsensical answer. Zak said that his dad was just afraid to handle my kind of case. I was the wrong color and drug defendants are politically unpopular. Bad for the firm's image, you know. Zak told me he would never forgive his father. I can understand that."

"How do you know Zak?" I shifted gears slightly.

"We met at a party during my first term. I was kind of over to one corner, drinking a beer by myself. I think he felt sorry for me. I didn't care. I was just happy to have someone to talk to. He was really sweet and charming and funny. He was different, you know, not macho, not interested in impressing me or anything. We dated for a few months. We even lived together for a week," she laughed. "That went kind of rough, so we chilled for a while."

"Did you get back together?"

"Didn't get the chance." She tugged on her jail fatigues. "Zak and I thought it was a good idea to give it a rest for a few weeks. We agreed to talk about it as soon as we got back from Spring break. He flew back home a couple of days early and I went skiing before driving to Conn—"

"Skiing!" MacClough perked up.

"Yes, skiing." She was indignant. "All the basketball courts were taken."

"That's not what he means," I interrupted. "Were you arrested on your way back from skiing?"

"I was."

"And if I guess where it was you went skiing, will you promise to have a little hope?"

"You ever been chained to a chair, Mr. Klein? It's hard to have hope when you're chained to a chair."

"Point well taken." I paused. "Cyclone Ridge."

She didn't react at all the way I had expected. "So what?" she said. "You could've found that out fifty different ways. You could have read it in the paper."

"The point is that he didn't," MacClough jumped to my defense.

"Don't you think my lawyer sent an investigator up there? They didn't find anything. What do you think you'll find almost a year after the fact?"

"Show her the paper," John gestured to me.

I unfurled a copy of the Riversborough Gazette article about Steven Markum's death. "Recognize him?"

Her eyes got wide. "He was . . ." She choked up. "He was the valet."

"I think," MacClough said, "we just found out how that Isotope got into your car."

"But he's dead," Valencia Jones was quick to note. "What good does that do me?"

"Maybe none," John confessed. "But if I were you, I might find a way to get conveniently sick for a few days. I also think I can foresee your lawyer getting the urge to file every motion she can think of. I'd say it was in your best interest to stretch things out, if you catch my drift."

We spent the remainder of our time with Valencia Jones talking directly about Zak's disappearance. She was as clueless on the subject as everyone else. She did, however, recommend that we look up some cyberfreak friend of Zak's called Guppy. She didn't know his real name or address, but that his hacking exploits were the stuff of campus legend. Just for the hell of it, I wondered if Zak had ever mentioned a girl named Kira Wantanabe? Valencia Jones said the name was unfamiliar to her, but that she didn't know all of Zak's friends.

There was a thunderous knock on the steel door. It swung open. The prison matron leaned into the room and shouted: "Time!"

We did a quick round of farewells. Just before I was at the door, Valencia Jones called to me. I turned.

"Even if this doesn't work out for me," she said, "I hope you find Zak."

"Thanks."

And as I watched the guard unshackle Valencia Jones' leg, I thought I saw something that looked like hope in the corners of her eyes.

Paper Apologies

We didn't speak much on the ride back to Riversborough. MacClough was busy absorbing information and planning our next moves. My mind was just as busy, but my thoughts were far more scattered. I was furious with Jeffrey for not telling us about Zak's connection to Valencia Jones. At the same time, I had a gut feeling that John and I were on the verge of stumbling onto something very big. Unfortunately, I couldn't see how any of this was getting us closer to finding Zak. Traces of Zak were all around the periphery, but it was Valencia Jones at the center of this part of the universe.

It was past dusk when MacClough pulled into the rest stop where I had left my rental. As I was getting out of the car, John grabbed my arm.

"You can see now that you had nothing to do with Markum's death, can't you?"

"I guess," I said, "but I still feel like shit."

"Come on, Klein, think! This is bigger than Steven Markum. I can't tell you for sure, but I would bet Valencia Jones wasn't the only person whose car got packed with a little extra baggage. With the trial coming up, Markum's old employers probably didn't want to risk him opening his mouth. He was going down whether you got chucked in that holding cell with him or not. So stop beating yourself up over it."

"Is that what you're doing with the Boatswain case," I wondered, "beating yourself up over it?"

"Yeah." MacClough shook his head, "I saw that fax in your room. But believe me, even your big *macher* friend Feld doesn't understand. So don't you try to. You'll find out soon enough."

"What does that mean?"

He ignored me. "Get some sleep. I think we need some skiing lessons."

The door wasn't fully closed, but he pulled away just the same. The sleeve buttons of the peacoat caught on the door edge, shredding the coat arm as it went.

*   *   *

I picked up some fast food and went back to the Old Watermill. I was so preoccupied that I nearly didn't notice who was behind the desk. My old pal was on duty.

"How was ice fishing?" I teased.

"Huh?" he puzzled.

"Never mind. Can I have a word with you?" The way I said it, it didn't sound like a question. I stepped into the vacant guest lounge. He followed, but without much bounce in his step. "Okay. Now you want to explain your rudeness to me the other morning? Or do you always treat people like shit who give you big tips?"

"It wasn't you," he raised his hand as if to swear an oath. "It was. . . um . . . It was . . . you know."

"The girl I was with?"

"You said it. But anyway, yes. We don't usually let her kind in here."

I was so stunned by his admission that it took me a few seconds to lift him into the air by his neck. He was even more stunned and his face turned several shades of red. I told him he'd have a career as a color chart for flesh-tone paints, if I let him live.

"You don't understand," he managed to choke out. "She's a—"

I squeezed a little harder. "She's a what, asshole? Come on, cat got your tongue?"

When his eyes began rolling up in his head, I relaxed my grip and let him down. He gasped, grabbing at his throat. He coughed up phlegm and fell to his knees.

"Listen, you racist motherfucker," I began, "I'll cut your heart—"

"That's not what I meant," he said, his voice stronger now. "She's a pro. This is a respectable place. It's against house rules to let working girls up to the rooms. I could have lost my job."

And somewhere, deep in my belly, I knew he was telling the truth. I helped him to his feet. The, "How do you know that for sure?" came out of my mouth reflexively.

"There's this place over the border. A, um. . . Anyway,

there's a place over there where they throw these way cool bachelor parties. Theme parties, you know? The bachelor chooses the theme and for like a C-note and a half a guy, they send you around the world."

"Okay, I'm sold, but get to the point. What about the girl?"

"My friend's party was there. His theme was to get stranded with a native girl. She was—"

"—the native girl," I finished. "You're sure?"

"Trust me, Mr. Klein, I wouldn't forget her. She—"

"Spare me the details."

I pulled five hundred dollars of Jeffrey's money out of my wallet. I put the bills in the clerk's palm and told him it was just my way of saying sorry for nearly killing him. He said he preferred paper apologies and that anytime I wanted to work off a little tension at five hundred bucks per minute, to just ring him at the desk. I informed him that the money came with a catch. He had to keep quiet about the girl and he had to let her keep coming up to my room. He didn't like that so much. I could see him begin to waver. And when he moved his hand to return the five bills, I grabbed his wrist.

"Give me a few days. There's another five hundred in it for you and we can leave out the rough stuff this time. Just look the other way when the girl comes in and goes out. Half a grand to look the other way is pretty easy money. Deal?" I let go of his wrist.

He hesitated. Then shoved the money in his pocket. "Deal."

I was curious. "Anybody else who works here know about her?"

"I don't think so."

"Good. Keep it that way."

I let him walk back to his station at the front desk. After taking a minute to consult the local Yellow Pages, I headed back into the night. Before I got out the door, I literally ran into MacClough. Judging by the bags he dropped at my feet, he too had decided on fast food for dinner.

"Where you going?" he whispered, as I knelt down to pick up his food.

"To take a test," I whispered back. "Wish me luck."

Clearly confused, John stood stony-faced as I played the part of the clumsy stranger. I apologized profusely for knocking into him. I think the desk clerk was watching to see how much money I would slip MacClough. John reluctantly let me go with a warning to be a little more careful in the future. At the time, John had no way of knowing just how ironic that bit of advice was.

Peekaboo

I knew one of them would be waiting for me when I got back. I was glad it wasn't Kira, if that was her name. I don't know how I would have handled that. Ripping her heart out seemed fair. I could hear the interrogation now.

"Why'd ya do it, Klein?"

"I was looking for a hooker with a heart of gold."

I wanted to tear my own hair out, I had been so stupid. Why hadn't I listened to my own suspicions? I cursed my own vanity, my insecurities. And for some reason, at that moment, I found myself missing my father. It was an unfamiliar feeling. During his life, he had not been the type of man to be missed. His anger, his bitterness had seen to that. Who would miss me, I wondered? Who would miss *me*?

The TV was on and MacClough was passed out on my bed when I came in. He looked tense these days, even in sleep. I noticed he was dreaming. His fingers and legs jerked. His eyeballs rolled frantically beneath his lids. He kept mumbling something that sounded like I'm sorry. He wasn't the only one. It was a night for being sorry. Some nights you fry fish. Some nights you're sorry.

He was up when I got out of the shower and busy worrying a bald spot in the carpet. He wanted to know what that mumbo jumbo was that I had whispered about taking a test. I detailed my conversation with the desk clerk. MacClough didn't bother calling Kira names. He had been a cop too long to get indignant about prostitution. To him, it was a business not too unlike most others. There were users and people who got used. Sometimes it was hard to tell them apart.

"How long before you get the results?"

"You know," I laughed, "I didn't ask. Having the test done was stupid, anyway. It'ss take weeks for me to develop HIV antibodies if I'm infected. I guess I just panicked."

"Yeah, I never thought I'd ever look back at worrying about the clap as the good old days, but Christ almighty, it's a nightmare out there now."

"Tell me about it."

"Listen," he said, "I don't think you've got anything to worry about."

"Thanks, John, but—"

"Hear me out, schmuck. If she's a high-ticket girl, her employers have a vested interest in keeping her healthy. She's a valuable commodity. She probably gets tested all the time. Besides, whoever put her close to you wants you outta town as soon as possible and wants you to stay out. Why risk getting you sick and coming back here dredging up all kinds of shit? It's stupid and from what I've seen so far, I don't think we're dealing with idiots. Crime works best when nobody notices it. Sound reasonable to you?"

"Sounds like a rationalization," I winked, "but thanks."

"Yeah, well, maybe it is." He hesitated a bit before speaking again. "You know you've got to let her keep coming here. If she finds out her cover is blown, we're fucked. Her employers will close down shop and we won't find jack shit."

"I know, John."

"I'm just worried about you, Klein."

"That's funny," I said. "I've been pretty worried about you lately. When I came in here, you were having a bad dream. You were twitching like mad and mumbling, 'I'm sorry.' What's wrong? Does this have anything to do with the Boatswain-Hernandez thing?"

"You're right, I *was* having a bad dream." His whole face smiled but for his eyes. "I dreamed I was asking a Jewish girl to marry me and she thought the five carat ring I bought her wasn't big enough. You bet I was saying I was sorry."

"Get the fuck out of here, you antiSemite."

"I'm not antiSemitic," he protested, "I only hate you. Now get some sleep. The slopes await us." He closed the door behind him.

I dialed both Larry Feld's office and home numbers and got two machines. I hung up twice without leaving messages. After the second hang up, I dutifully went through the motions of going to sleep. I spent the rest of the time till sunup playing peekaboo with every bad decision I had ever made.

Coney Island Burning

Larry Feld was unhappy. That was par for the course. His parents had set a good example. Today he was unhappy about answering phone calls at sunrise. He was unhappy I had waited so long to get back to him after his fax. But what made him most unhappy—and this, of course, went unsaid—was the prospect that I no longer needed him or his dirty little stories.

I was usually amenable to playing the game his way: answering his questions, letting him gloat when I got things wrong. I wasn't in the mood today. I didn't know that I'd ever be in the mood again. I was scared for Zak. I was scared for myself, too scared to play straight man to Larry Feld's wounded ego or to stroke the lost little boy that would live inside him forever. I had done enough of that when we were kids. And when he began interrogating me about his fax, I told him to forget it. He was either going to tell me about Boatswain-Hernandez or he wasn't, but I wasn't going to play.

"No, Dylan, it doesn't work that way."

"Larry!"

"Sorry," he said without feeling. "But let me ask you something. Do you remember what your brother did straight out of law school?"

"He was an assistant district attorney in the Bronx. So what?"

Feld didn't answer that. He just said, "Go read your first book and put two and two together. Even you can get to four."

"I'm not in the mood for this, Larry."

"The next time you ask a question, make sure you're ready to hear the answer."

He hung up before I could say another word. I tried in vain to muster some enthusiasm for going to Cyclone Ridge with MacClough. Giving up, I rang John's room and begged out. He said he understood and that I would probably have just gotten in his way. He was right. In the shape I was in, I was of no use to anyone, particularly myself. I closed my eyes and, more out of the need for escape than exhaustion, I fell deeply into dreamless sleep.

I got up around noon and noticed the message light on my phone was flashing red. I buzzed the desk. Kira had stopped by to say she would see me tonight around 8:00. I didn't like it. It didn't feel right. She had always played the guessing game with me; would she show up or wouldn't she? Why, I wondered, the change in tactics. Maybe she wanted to show me how much I was missed. Maybe she got paid extra for that.

Without trying to lose my entourage, I took a walk about campus and asked around for Guppy. Like Valencia Jones, everyone seemed to know about Guppy's reputation. No one seemed to know him or how to get in touch with him. Guppy was the kind of guy who gets in touch with you. One kid told me that he had heard that Guppy lived in the tunnels beneath campus. I asked the kid if he had taken his meds today.

Having struck out on my hunt for the great Guppy, I went over to the Riversborough public library and sat down with a copy of my first book, *Coney Island Burning*. Ich! It was really hard reading my own work, especially the early stuff. So I read the liner notes and hoped I would get whatever it was Larry Feld had hinted at. They went like this:

> While looking into the suspicious death of an old basketball buddy, insurance investigator Wyatt Rosen finds himself trapped in a racial firestorm. With New York City's African-American community ready to explode, Rosen, along with his best friend—ex-NYPD detective Timmy O'Shea—race against the clock to prove his old friend's murder was a crime of passion, not police brutality.

> In their quest, Rosen and O'Shea are forced to enlist an unlikely cast of characters including a radical black preacher, a Hasidic rabbi and a reformed underworld hitman. Rosen and O'Shea spend as much of their time juggling the diverse agendas and personalities of their team as they do fighting against the political and social forces aligned against them.

Rosen and O'Shea lock horns with Janson Whitehurst, an ambitious assistant district attorney who will stop at nothing to further his career, and his band of loyal toadies. There is nonstop action as O'Shea goes undercover to weed out the bad cop whose greed and carelessness opened this Pandora's box of ill-gotten gains, backroom deals and murder.

Along the way, Rosen runs into his first love and desperately seeks to rekindle the romance he had turned his back on years ago. Come for the ride as O'Shea confronts the man he is convinced is responsible for the death of his former partner, Jack Spinner, but who may also hold the fate of the city in his grasp.

At its core, *Coney Island Burning* is a hard-boiled novel with a 90s edge . . .

I didn't get it, not right away. I braced myself and began turning past the title page, past the copyright, past the dedication and acknowledgments to the first chapter. Then, I'm not certain I know what made me do it, but I turned back to the dedication and acknowledgments. And there were their names, separated by only a few lines:

"For my brothers, Jeffrey and Josh, who showed me that heroes can have clay feet and still stand tall.

I would like to thank my friend and technical advisor, John MacClough, for his inspiration and support."

I tried remembering the date of the Boatswain kidnapping. March of '72, I seemed to recall. That would put my assistant district attorney brother and uniformed police officer John MacClough in the Bronx at the same time. They had never actually denied knowing each other. I had always just assumed they did not and they let me assume. I wanted to believe I was simply jumping to conclusions, that they *had* never met before I introduced them, but I knew it wasn't so. Larry Feld was a lot of things, but inaccurate wasn't one of them. There had to be a connection.

In my head, I ran through the parts of the plot of *Coney Island Burning* I could remember. Other than the obvious and superficial resemblance between my brother and the A.D.A. in my book, I was at a— That's when it hit me; MacClough had suggested the character of Janson Whitehurst, the corrupt A.D.A. He wasn't my invention. I tried recalling the other sections of the book John had suggested. Feverishly, I thumbed through the pages to the section where a dirty cop tortures information out of and then kills a drug dealer:

". . . hit him again and again in the kidneys with a tightly rolled newspaper. Gonzales stubbornly refused to give in, furiously shaking his head no.

"Tough spic, huh? Big *cojones*. Okay, macho man," Murphy said, patting his prisoner affectionately on the cheek. "We'll see about that."

Murphy reached not for his service revolver, but pulled up his pant leg to reveal a short-barrel .38. Smiling broadly, he unholstered the gun from his ankle, pulled back the hammer and put the barrel to Gonzales's temple. Murphy loosened the gag in the dealer's mouth and let it fall to the floor. Gonzales gasped for air.

"*Agua*," he coughed, "water."

"Here's something to put in your mouth." Murphy snapped Gonzales' head back by yanking on his thick, black ponytail and moved the gun barrel from his prisoner's temple into his mouth. He began to count: "Five . . . four . . . three . . . two . . . one.

"Okay, okay," Gonzales relented, sweat pouring down his face.

Murphy pulled the barrel back slightly so Gonzales could speak more clearly. "Go ahead, spic."

"The money is in employee locker 12 in Nathans' back room."

"You bullshitting me, *pendejo*?"

"I'm in no position to bullshit you."

Murphy smiled again. "I guess you're right."

As Gonzales began to smile with relief, Murphy shoved the .38 back into the dealer's mouth and calmly blew his brains out the rear of his skull. Murphy wiped the gun clean, untied the dead man's hands and wrapped the fingers of Gonzales' right hand around the handle of the little .38.

Using an untraceable second gun to make an unrighteous kill or just plain murder look like suicide was a time-honored trick. You wouldn't find the second gun trick in any manual or textbook, but it was one of those things old school cops learned before they ever set foot out of the academy.

Murphy continued the setup, wiping the whole house clean of his prints and making sure he took the rope, the gag and the newspaper with him. He really wasn't worried about getting prosecuted, not with his connection in the D.A.'s office. In a day or two, Murphy would drop a dime and make like an anonymous tipster. By that time, no one would connect him to Gonzales' death."

I was nauseous. MacClough had nearly dictated that part of the book to me. It seemed so real to me then, I hardly played with it. Now I knew there was a good reason for that. I could feel myself getting dizzy.

"You all right, sir?" A librarian shook me by the shoulder. "You don't look well."

I didn't answer. I stood up and stumbled up a half flight of stairs. When I looked back, I noticed the librarian studying my picture on the rear of the dust jacket. I smiled. It was a hollow smile.

*   *   *

After wandering around snowy Riversborough, I found myself drinking coffee in the coffee house I'd gone to with Kira a few days before. It seemed like quite a long time ago to me now. I laughed at myself, but no one was there to hear it. The waiter was in the back and there were no bongos or bad poetry at this hour of the day. I read the graffiti carved into the table for entertainment.

"Excuse me," a melodic voice interrupted my reading, "but I was wondering if I might have a seat with you? I do not enjoy my afternoon tea alone and you look so much like a friend of mine."

"I do?" I said, looking up into the dark, sweet face of a man of undetermined years. His hair was shiny and black, as were his eyes. I thought he might be Indian or Pakistani, maybe an Arab. "Sure, have a seat. What's your friend's name?"

"Oh," he smiled and sat, "that is of no matter. He is lost to me and speaking his name will not bring him back."

"Don't I know it."

"You too have lost someone?" he wondered.

"I hope not. I'm still looking."

"That is as it should be. Keep searching. A man searching may find many things, unexpected things."

"Some unexpected things can kill a man."

"Maybe so," my table mate agreed. "But they can enrich him as well."

"I didn't catch your name." I put my hand out. "Dylan Klein."

He shook my hand, his eyes checking his watch. "Oh dear, look at the time. I must excuse myself."

"Hey, what about your tea?" I called after him.

"Tea, I never drink the stuff. Keep searching. Maybe you will find my friend as well. Good day to you." He hurried out the door.

Pretty bizarre, I thought, pretty fucking bizarre, but why should afternoon coffee be any different from the rest of my life? When the waiter came to refill my cup, I described my philosophical friend and asked if he knew the man.

"Sounds like Rajiv Gupta," the waiter said without hesitation. "He's a clerk over at the campus bookstore. Nice guy."

"Guppy!" I said aloud, but to myself. "Everybody's got clues but no answers."

I walked some more, made a second stop at the library, and
headed back to the inn with the moon rising over my shoulder. Hesitating outside the door, I blew a good-night kiss to
my escorts in the blue minivan. I was almost getting used to
having them around. Truth was, they had kept their distance
today, not interfering with me as I strolled the
Riversborough campus hunting for Guppy. Maybe they were
waiting for me to slug a lady professor. I could see no one on
the street fitting the descriptions MacClough had given me
of the ski dude or the federal agent. Then again, they were
trying not to be seen.

"Dylan!" Kira rushed up to me, hugging me. "God, I've
missed you."

And for a second, I lit up. My heart raced. My cheeks
warmed. I could feel the smile on my face. In spite of everything I knew about her, it was undeniable that part of me
missed her as well. Not all of me though. I felt my smile
harden, the blood rushing out of my face.

"Is everything all right?" she wondered, trying to look
through me. "You don't seem yourself."

"No," I said, "I'm not all right."

Jesus, she was good. Her voice quivered: "Is it Zak?"

"No, it's not Zak. I just found out today that a friend I
thought I knew, I didn't really know at all."

And the moment I spoke the words, I wanted to take
them back. But like my mom used to say, once the words
leave your mouth, you're no longer their master. It was the
only truly wise thing she had ever said. I had been speaking
of MacClough, of course, though Kira could have inter-
preted my words as meant for her. If she had taken it that
way, her face didn't betray her.

"I'm sorry," she said right on cue.

Trying to assure her that my words were not a warning,
I pulled her by the hand into the ever-vacant guest lounge.
Making sure that we were alone, I kissed her deeply. While
pulling her hair back with my left hand, I slipped my right
into her coat, under her sweater, and began massaging her

left nipple. It hardened and I wondered how she had learned to fake that. She clamped her legs around my tight thigh and began sliding her groin up and down the length of my upper leg. Finally, she clamped down hard and shook the both of us.

And then, oddly, as if trying to convince me of her genuine attraction, she pulled my hand out of her sweater and pushed it onto the wet crotch of her blue jeans. She waited a few seconds before urging my fingers into her mouth. I no longer had any doubt why her employers had picked her to get close to me. The desk clerk said they paid the girls across the border a C-note and a half. I was willing to bet she came more dearly.

"I missed you, too," I confessed. "And I'd like more than anything to take you upstairs and let you wear me out, but . . . It's gotta be tomorrow night. I'm sorry. There's just some stuff I've got to work out by myself."

Not wanting to overplay her hand, she said, "I understand. I'm sorry that you've been hurt."

"I'll live."

"I hope so." She winked. "Be in your room tomorrow night and maybe I will come."

I walked her out to the lobby. My thousand dollar friend at the front desk was trying too hard to ignore us; whistling, checking and rechecking the empty mail slots. I wanted to smack him. As I leaned over to kiss Kira, I noticed John's image reflected in the glass door. I could make out his rugged features perfectly: the twinkling blue eyes, the crooked smile, the square jaw. Over the past decade, I had come to know his face as well as my own. Somehow that face looked different to me tonight there in the glass, but it wasn't MacClough who had changed. John MacClough had had nearly a quarter century to live with what he had done. I had lived with it for only a few hours.

"You really are someplace else tonight, aren't you?" There was that concern in her voice again.

"Yes." I pecked her on the cheek.

She walked out the door. When it swung shut, MacClough's reflection was gone. It was time to go speak with the man himself.

He wasn't in my room. I walked up to his. As I walked in, he handed me a cold bottle of my favorite ale. I took half the bottle in a gulp, but could not make my eyes meet his. He was easier to deal with as a reflection, when I could see him and see through him all at once.

"How was skiing?"

He said he hadn't done much of it. He had done a lot of hanging out at the bar, walking the grounds, bullshitting with the help. That was John in his glory. If you spent ten minutes with him over a beer, you'd understand why he had been so good at getting confessions out of suspects. I suppose he saved the rolled-up newspaper for special cases.

"Markum worked there, all right," MacClough said. "Two years. He was a jack-of-all-trades. He worked on the lifts some, waited tables, but mostly parked cars. Wanna guess when he got fired?"

My head was spinning. "No."

"The day after Valencia Jones was arrested. You think somebody was a little pissed at him for planting the Isotope on the wrong car?"

"I guess," I said. "But he's been floating around loose for a year. Why kill him now?"

"From what I found out about Markum, no one was gonna beat down his door with job offers. Maybe he figured with the trial coming up he could put the squeeze on his old bosses for a little hush money. Getting killed is a kinda tough way to learn that blackmail isn't so easy as they make it on the tube."

"Anything else? Anything about Zak?"

"Nothing about your nephew. Sorry. But there were a few buildings up there I'd like to get into to have a look-see." He turned the tables: "And you, what'd you do? Did you get the test results?"

I explained that I hadn't, that I had other things on my mind.

"Other things!" He was incredulous. "You're waiting for the results of a fucking AIDS test, what else could you have on your mind?"

"Don't ask the question unless you're prepared to hear the answer," I paraphrased Larry Feld's earlier admonition.

He let that go without a word, pressing me about my day. Omitting my call to Feld and my two side trips to the public library, I laid it out for him. I told him about the coffee house and my visitation by the mythical Guppy. I related our conversation as close to verbatim as I could manage without a transcript. MacClough was keen to know what I thought it meant.

"At first, at the coffee house, I didn't think it meant anything," I said. "Just another interested party weighing in with well wishes and vague hints of this or that. But as I went over it in my head, it seemed to me he was delivering some kind of coded message. I don't know."

"You think he knows something?"

"It was weird, John. It was as if he wanted me to know he was delivering a message, but not to realize it until after he had gone. And his demeanor was so calm, unworried, like he wanted to reassure me. But if he knows something, why didn't he come right out and say it?"

"Maybe," MacClough suggested, "you didn't meet Guppy at all."

"But I did."

"How do you know? Come on, Klein, use that *yiddisha kop* God gave you," he said with a perfect accent, slapping my forehead. "How do you know what Guppy looks like? Interesting, isn't it? You walk around campus all morning asking about Guppy, but no one knows who he is or where he lives or how to reach him. Then, bang! Three hours later, Guppy serves himself up to you on a silver platter. All you know is that you had a weird conversation with a guy named Rajiv Gupta and you can't even be sure of that."

"Guppy the red herring. Great title for a children's book, you think?"

"If they could put the girl next to you, they could just as easily dig up a clown to talk some shit to you, confuse you, throw you off the scent."

"About the girl . . ." I was almost glad MacClough had broached the subject. "I don't think I can play my part much longer. And tonight, when you saw us down in the lobby, I think she might have suspected something was different."

"I know it's hard when you're that angry at someone," he empathized.

I laughed at him for that. "It's not the anger that makes it hard, John. It's the lack of it."

"She's that convincing, that good?"

"She's better. She's opaque. When I kiss her, when I look into her eyes, I can't believe she's acting. God, I'll be glad to be away from this place."

"Okay, one more performance." MacClough rubbed my shoulder. "We'll feed her a little misinformation to take back to her masters. Two can play these games."

"You would know, wouldn't you, John? You and my brother Jeff."

"And what's that supposed to mean?"

I did not want to believe the words that next came out of my mouth:

"You killed Hernandez and Jeff helped you cover it up."

"No, Klein, that's what you think you know."

"It's what I know!"

"Who told you so?" he sneered.

"You did, John."

I reached under my coat and produced the copy of *Coney Island Burning* I had stolen from the public library on my way back to the Old Watermill. I handed the book to MacClough.

It was his turn to laugh. "If it was that simple, I wouldn't hate myself so much."

"Then explain it to me. Make me understand."

"You'll understand soon enough," he repeated the words he had said to me at the rest stop.

Soon enough could not come soon enough for me.

He left a note for me. He had to get back downstate to take care of some personal business and to check on the Rusty Scupper. I did not pretend to myself that I wasn't relieved. He wrote that he had stayed up all night doing the reading I had suggested. He had nothing to say on the subject of my brother or of their mutual involvement with Boatswain-Hernandez. Parroting my review in *Publishers Weekly*, however, MacClough commented that he found *Coney Island Burning* a captivating character study featuring crisp, staccato dialogue, but that the plot was rather too arcane and my attempt to bridge the gap between the hard-boiled genre and today's suspense thriller was only sporadically successful. I marveled at the man. I marveled at his ability to remember that review and how it had seemed to hurt him more than me. I marveled at his ability to hang onto his sense of humor. I was not at all certain that I would be able to.

I had met killers before; some on my own, some with Johnny's help. I had shared food and drinks with, told dirty jokes to, and played poker with murderers. I had even listened to some describe with cold precision every detail of their crimes. Had it bothered me? Yeah, I guess, a little, but their crimes were as remote to me as the crimes I wrote about in my fiction. The killers themselves were two-dimensional cartoon characters; evil somehow, but unreal.

Well, I was a hypocrite, because it was different with MacClough. None of those other men were my best friend. John was. None had risked his life to save mine. John had. I barely remembered those mens' faces. I knew John's face better than my own. He was as close to me as a brother. No, closer. We understood one another better than brothers do. I used to think so. I wasn't quite as sure now. Maybe it was a measure of the world's unending barrage of cruelty that murder only mattered when it hit close to home. More likely, it was a measure of my own weakness. If what I thought was true, that John had killed Hernandez in cold blood, I knew I would never be able to look at him in the same way again.

And I would have two men to mourn after this mess was over.

It was with this black heart that I set out for breakfast.

The coffee shop was crowded with students and I had to wait about ten minutes to be seated. I used the down time to thumb through the *Gazette*. Steven Markum was already old news. Mention of his "accidental" death was nowhere to be found. The Valencia Jones trial, on the other hand, remained a hot topic. The headline at the top of the third page let me know that Ms. Jones and her lawyer had taken our advice to heart:

JONES FALLS ILL—TRIAL ON HOLD

The article went on to explain that the judge agreed to interrupt the trial to allow Ms. Jones sufficient time to recover from what a leery prosecutor, Robert W. Smart termed: "Her sudden and convenient ailment." The trial judge also noted that the time off would allow him to deal with the flurry of motions Ms. Jones' attorney had filed in recent days. It was clear from the story that neither judge nor prosecutor was very pleased with these obvious delaying tactics. And, though neither stated it for the record, it was equally clear that Valencia Jones would pay a price for stalling. I hoped we would be able to make it worth the gamble.

By the time I had finished off a pot of coffee and one cholesterol special—two scrambled eggs, cheese and bacon on a buttered roll—the place had cleared out. My waitress was the chatty woman who had gossiped about the death up at Cyclone Ridge to Kira and me. She hadn't been so talkative this morning; not enough blood in the morning paper to suit her purposes. But I was as wrong about her as I was about most everything else.

"Where's your girlfriend, honey?" she asked me right out. And when I hesitated, she prompted: "You know, that cute oriental number you was in with the other morning?"

"She's not my girlfriend," was the best I could manage.

"Too bad."

"How's that?"

"Well, she's in here a lot, usually solo." The gossip

shook her head in dismay. "And the few times I seen her in here with a fella, it's most a the time some dorky college kid. It's a pity, a cute girl like that."

"She's a regular?" I wondered.

"Twice a week since her freshman year."

Freshman year, my ass. I bit my lip not to say it. Kira probably came into the coffee shop after hard nights turning tricks on campus for a little mad money. And for an extra twenty bucks, she'd let you take her to breakfast. I felt the corners of my mouth curl into a nasty smile.

When my eyes refocused on the waitress, she was staring hard at me.

"Something the matter?"

Wagging her finger at me: "You look real familiar to me. I thought so the other day, too, but I couldn't place you. Where the hell do I know you from?"

"Read any detective novels?"

"Never. I'm a Harlequin romance gal myself."

"Go to Brooklyn College?"

"Honey, the closest I ever want to get to Brooklyn is watching reruns of *Welcome Back Kotter* on TV."

"You ever get down to Long—"

"That's it!" she snapped her fingers. "You look just like one of the boys that oriental girl used to come in here with. You his father?"

I shut the busybody out before she finished her question. What she said about the boy who looked like me didn't make any sense, if that boy was Zak. Even if Kira really did turn tricks on campus, her new employers would never have risked using her to get close to me; too many variables. They could never be sure Zak hadn't discussed her with me over a beer or in the locker room. A kid might not talk to his father about going to a hooker, but you couldn't be sure he wouldn't tell a favorite uncle. And if they were willing to wager Zak hadn't told me, they couldn't take the chance of some other customer recognizing her as she walked around Riversborough at my side.

"This the boy?" I showed her my wallet photo of Zak.

"That's him. Sorry about that dorky college boy crack."

"It's forgotten. Listen, this girl we're talking about, you ever catch her name?"

She was staring at me again. Why would I have to ask the name of someone I obviously knew?

"I know it's a weird question, but humor me, please?"

"Well, mister, I ain't the nosy type," she said with a straight face.

"Oh, believe me, I know you're not. It's just that I worked as a waiter myself for a while and I overheard things I wasn't trying to eavesdrop on. Come on . . . Sandra," I read her name tag. "As a favor to an old waiter, try and remember."

Sandra screwed up her face for dramatic effect, but I don't imagine she had to search her memory for more than a nanosecond. "Kiwi, Keela, I don't know, foreign sounding like that."

"Kira?"

"Sounds about right," she nodded. "Can I get you anything else?"

I waved a fifty-dollar bill under her nose. "Is there a way out of this place other than the front door?"

"Through the kitchen, into an alley that leads to Beethoven Street."

I handed Sandra the fifty. "Think you can arrange a tour of the kitchen for me?"

"For a handsome man like yourself," Sandra purred, leering at me in a way she must have thought sexy, "I could arrange almost anything."

"I might just take you up on that." I kissed the back of her hand. "But for now, let's see about the back door."

With the fifty bucks worth of consolation, Sandra disappeared into the kitchen. She reappeared at my table within two minutes. Everything was arranged. I left a five on the table to cover breakfast.

"Listen," I whispered to her as I stood up, "make like you're pointing the way to the bathroom." She did. "Great. Some men are going to come in asking about me in a few minutes. Whatever you do, swear to me that you won't tell them I'm going back downstate for a few days."

"I swear."

As I trotted down the alleyway towards Beethoven Street, my legs were fueled by hope. Hope wasn't something I was terribly familiar with, but it felt pretty damned fine. Now I needed some time, sans chaperones, to make certain my newfound hope wasn't of the false variety. My exit through the kitchen was a start. And since I figured Sandra the waitress would confess as to my fraudulent travel plans within five minutes, I thought I could count on at least a few hours of unfettered activity.

My first stop was a ski shop. I grabbed a new parka, gloves, a turtleneck, pants, and a pair of hiking shoes off the shelf. I bought a wool ski hat—I hated hats—and a pair of those orange reflector sunglasses that make you look like an alien with no fashion sense. I hardly recognized myself. I doubted if anyone else would, not at first glance. When the salesman offered to put my peacoat out of its misery, I snapped at him. I had him box the clothes I'd come in with and paid for them to be shipped back to Sound Hill.

I strolled over to the campus under a bright sun. It was relatively warm and, for the first time since I'd arrived, snow wasn't part of the forecast. That would help. Fewer students would be inclined to take the subterranean passageways between buildings. Now all I had to do was spot Kira and follow her without her noticing me. I took the high ground atop the library steps, watching.

Surveillance, boredom is thy name. I detested it. Hurry up and wait and wait and wait. It was the endless, often fruit-less hours of loneliness that had helped push me out of insur-ance investigations. It was all about cold nights in cold cars drinking cold coffee. I used to think that Eliot had gotten it all wrong, life wasn't about coffee spoons, but about coffee containers: *I have known the ins, outs, downs and ups, I have measured out my nights with coffee cups.*

But like MacClough used to say, "If you could quote T.S. fuckin' Eliot, you were in the wrong job anyway." He was right, of course.

I didn't have to look at my watch to know an hour had passed. After doing enough surveillance, you gain intimate knowledge of the passage of time, the deathly slow march of it. Only in retrospect does time ever pass quickly. Besides, I was standing under the clock tower and the chimes were kind of hard to ignore.

By the second round of chimes, my more usual sense of pessimism had set in. I would never find Kira this way. For all I knew, she didn't have class today. And I knew nothing for sure. For chrissakes, maybe she *was* an expensive hooker. I couldn't recall the last time I felt so unsure of myself. I had forfeited control of my emotional life to desk clerks and chatty waitresses. I was so far removed from my original purpose that I doubted the value of getting involved. These things, I thought, were better left to hard men, men not so easily distracted.

I was on the downward spiral of negativity followed by self-recrimination. The anger and explosion would not be far behind. "Thanks Dad!" I said, wishing he could hear me. Noticing I was cold, I deserted my spot on the granite steps of the library.

The cafeteria wasn't too difficult to find without a map. I poured myself the biggest container of coffee I could find. The fat, unsmiling woman at the register shook her head no at me.

"What's the matter?" I gritted my teeth.

"That's a soda container you got there. Can't take coffee out of here in a soda container."

"Charge me for it."

"Can't do that," she explained. "Gotta get a coffee container."

"Here's five bucks, charge me whatever you want."

"Can't do—

"—that. Yeah, yeah, yeah."

I left the coffee at the register and started for Dean Dallenbach's office. I hadn't wanted to go through him to find out about Kira, but now I didn't see that I had a choice. I was wrong.

There she was, fifty feet in front of me, a distressed leather book bag strapped to her back. I slowed my pace and fell in behind a crowd of students arguing the merits of the Categorical Imperative. Wasn't liberal arts grand? I hoped none of these kids planned on working for a living. As she moved, I moved. She came to rest in the third row, third seat from the front of room 203 of Snodgras Hall.

I couldn't hear the lecture through the closed door, but figured it was an English class of some form or another. The professor's salt-and-pepper hair was too long, falling on the shoulders of his green corduroy jacket. He strutted about, waving his arms like a hackneyed Hamlet, his eyes never straying too far from the prettiest women in class. I'd taken enough English courses to know that most literature professors were just frustrated actors with ids the size of Chicago. Okay, maybe some were frustrated writers. Id size remained constant.

At the end of the lecture I ducked into a nearby doorway and picked up on my shadowing routine. It went on like that until late in the afternoon. It wasn't all bad, though. I did rather enjoy the live models in Kira's sketching class. When the instructor shooed them out of the art room, I watched Kira disappear around a bend in the hallway. I failed to see the point in following her any longer. What would watching her sit through one more class prove? Yet, my doubts lingered. I was afraid to trust the obvious, that Kira was a student at Riversborough. I needed a little independent confirmation.

"Excuse me," I called to Kira's art instructor. "Can I have a word with you?"

"Sure." She waved me up to the front of the class. She was a smallish woman with close-cropped brown hair and copper brown eyes. She had hollow cheeks smudged with charcoal and a friendly smile.

"Hi," I put out my hand for a shake, but she showed me her blackened palms and we agreed that my gesture would suffice. "My name's Dylan Klein."

"Jane Courteau. What can I do for you, Mr. Klein?"

"I write books, detective novels."

"I've never heard of you."

"You're in good company. Want to see my Authors Guild card?"

"I'll take your word for it," she said. "I'm supposed to be a talented artist and no one's ever heard of me. And we don't even get cards!"

"To tell you the truth, mine's expired. Anyway, I have some say over what the cover design of my next book will be and someone suggested one of your students as a potential artist," I lied. "I wanted to get your opinion first before I approached the student."

"Which student?"

"Kira Wantanabe."

Jane Courteau had trouble concealing her dismay. It wasn't exactly horror I saw flashing across her face, but it was more than a frown.

I played coy. "No good, huh?"

"She's not terrible."

"I admire a woman who rejects faint praise as an option."

"Look, Mr. Klein, what I mean to say is that Kira is competent. I've had her for three terms now and she's improved immensely, but she doesn't have her heart in it. I don't mean to insult her."

"It's our secret. No one's been hurt. Thank you," I gushed, barely able to contain myself.

"I have several other students I might suggest."

"That's okay," I assured her as I turned to leave. "If I go to anyone, it will be directly to you. I won't forget you."

Walking away, I realized I must've seemed quite the fool to Ms. Jane Courteau. I was a fool, a very happy and relieved fool. I stopped in the student lounge and called the lab from a pay phone. Although I couldn't vouch for Kira's activity before she met me, let's just say that much of the suspense had been taken out of the call. In a thoroughly disinterested voice, the attendant confirmed I was HIV negative. You always tell yourself that you'll deal with whatever happens, no matter how bad. But I'll confess to feeling such a high at that moment I could have kissed the pepper-spray boy right on the lips, Rush Limbaugh and Joe McCarthy not withstanding.

I bought two bottles of champagne at the liquor store. I intended to share the painted-flower bottle of Perrier-Jouet with Kira. I was undecided about the second, far less expensive bottle of Korbel. I was either going to send it to Jane Courteau without a note or use it as a fleet enema for the desk clerk at the Old Watermill Inn. I was thinking I'd been an idiot for listening to him. People get other people's faces mixed up all the time. He had probably been drunk out of his mind when he was across the border at his buddy's bachelor party. Then, like a kick in the groin I wasn't expecting, it hit me; maybe the desk clerk hadn't gotten it wrong at all. Maybe he was lying to me. I wondered about why he would do that. I'd have to have a chat with him on the subject when MacClough got back into town. I lacked John's wherewithal when it came to interviews.

Walking up the street, I noticed the blue minivan parked across the way from the inn. I approached from the rear and rapped hard on the passenger side window. The campus security guy nearly coughed up his glazed doughnut.

"Just checking in," I screamed through the rolled-up window. "Got back from downstate sooner than I thought."

He tried, and failed, to look unfazed by my abrupt return. It's tough to act cool with a chewed doughnut hanging out of your mouth. His partner in the driver's seat was considerably less worried about my opinion of things and gave me the finger. I respected that. He and doughnut-boy had more than likely gotten reamed for losing me. As a gesture of goodwill, I showed them the bottle of Korbel and left it on the sidewalk.

Once inside the Old Watermill, I continued acting like a smug jerk. I found my pal at the front desk. He put down his spy novel and gave me a knowing smile. But what did he know, I wondered? There were no messages for me.

"Listen, buddy," I whispered, "she's coming over tonight. Do me a favor and send her right up when she gets here, okay?"

"Sure thing, Mr. Klein."

"Anybody come in here today looking for me?"

"Nobody," he said, giving the boy scout salute.

I handed him the champagne. "You think you can have this chilled for me and have it sent up when my *date* gets here?"

"No problem."

I didn't give him a tip. He'd made all the money off me he was going to make.

The room was different somehow. I can't explain it. Hotel rooms aren't like your own place. I couldn't vouch for where I had put my dirty socks or what page the paper was turned to when I put it down before sleep. I didn't know what bugs hung out in the corners of the ceiling. I didn't know the smells or the sounds. And there was a cleaning service that came in every day to pick up after me, to make the bed, to fold the end of the toilet paper into a point. Even so, I could not shake the feeling that someone who did not belong had been in my room. But I also thought we'd have a colony on the moon by now.

As promised, he sent her right up. Even called me to let me know she was coming. I was glad to see Jeffrey's five hundred dollars hadn't gone totally to waste. Hey, for another hundred, maybe he would have escorted Kira to my room.

I was obviously grinning like an idiot when I opened the door.

"What?"

"You're what," I said, pulling her into my room by the wrist and kicking the door shut behind her.

I proceeded to kiss her until the air she breathed out was the air I breathed in, until I was drunk from it. Although I will likely remember that one kiss even after I'm dead, it wasn't overtly sexual. It was a kiss of joy, of relief; a kiss that hinted at the absence of love in my life. And when we finally let our lips pull apart, Kira hung her head.

"What is it?" I nudged her chin up with my finger.

She was crying, silently. Glistening streams ran over her translucent skin into the edges of her mouth. The tip of her tongue moved from side to side licking at the tears. I did not need to ask what the tears were for. If I had had the courage, I would have been crying, too.

"I am falling in love with you, Uncle Dylan. And last night, I was afraid. I could feel a wall around you, built to keep me out."

"There was a wall, but I didn't build it."

"I don't understand."

I told her everything. I had to. There was never a thought of holding back, though I realized she might've felt betrayed by my readiness to believe the worst of her. I explained that my disbelief in her said more about my life than hers. She did not flinch.

"Do you think he lied or just got it wrong?" Kira wanted to know.

"I'm not sure."

Laughing, she said: "Professor Courteau must have fainted when you told her about wanting to use my drawings for your next book."

"I had to call the paramedics."

Kira slapped me playfully. I pulled her close again. We fell onto the bed. When we came up for air, she was smiling up at me with a glint of mischief in her black eyes.

"What now?" I asked.

"Would I have been worth the hundred and fifty dollars the desk clerk claimed they charged for me?"

"More."

There was a knock on the door. It was room service with my chilled champagne. I shooed the waiter away with an overwhelming tip and a shove on the shoulder. I opened the champagne properly, holding the cork and twisting the bottle slowly. Kira had already helped herself to an empty flute which I filled with an inch of champagne and five inches of white foam. I didn't bother with a glass myself and we clinked bottle to flute.

Coyly, she wondered, "How much more would I be worth?"

"Back to that again?" I tried unsuccessfully to sneer at her. "I don't know, a buck and a quarter maybe."

She punched me in the arm, less playfully this time.

"Ouch!" I rubbed it. "Okay, I'll tell you how much more you're worth. You're worth the rest of my life. If I thought there was a chance you'd say yes, I'd ask you to marry me."

Her face went utterly blank. She knew I wasn't kidding.

"I'd like that," she whispered, curling her arms and legs about me. "Ask me."

"But I'm old enough—"

"—to make me happy."

"What about school?"

"I suddenly don't care much for Riversborough. Ask me, Dylan."

"Will you marry me?"

"Yes."

At that moment I wasn't thinking of love and the future, children and white picket fences. I was thinking of a movie, *The Day The Earth Stood Still*. There's this scene when Michael Rennie and Patricia Neal are trapped alone together in a darkened elevator as all the power in all the world is shut off for half an hour. And in that half hour, as the rest of the planet panics, Rennie and Neal, people literally from two different worlds, bond in a permanent, unspoken way. Even as a kid, before I understood anything about love and relationships, the power of their connection in that dark elevator got to me. I guess it's funny what you think about.

"Where are you?" Kira caught me drifting.

"Trapped on an elevator."

I never did get to explain that. Reaching back, she flicked off the lights. Taking a gulp of champagne, she kissed me, urging some of the wine into my mouth. I swallowed it. She kissed me again, softly, peeling back my denim shirt. She ran her tongue down along the hair of my chest. Kira cradled my left nipple between her lips, first sucking gently, then harder and harder still. I cupped the back of her head in my hand and pressed her lips against my chest. Sliding a petite hand along my abdomen, she undid my belt and button. With some persuasion, my pants and briefs fell to the floor.

Kira bit my nipple. She poured herself some more champagne, directly from the bottle this time, and dropped to her knees. She took me into her mouth. I got weak. The mixture of her hot breath and the cold wine against my skin was so overwhelming, my knees buckled. But I held back. I wanted to be inside her, holding her, not standing above her. My impending orgasm, however, would not afford me the leisure of taking it slow and easy. I pulled away and pulled her up, tearing at Kira's black silk blouse. The buttons ricocheted off the walls and windows like so many BBs. There was no brassiere to tangle with.

Sucking on her breasts, I worked her pants loose. She kicked them free of her legs as I rolled her onto the bed. I kissed her mouth, her painted red lips were dry with the fever of the moment. Her tongue forced its way between my teeth. She reached below my waist and pulled me into her. Her vagina was incredibly wet with excitement, so wet that I felt I could slide my soul inside her. Kira's back arched up. Her teeth took hold of my bottom lip and I tasted blood as I let go of forty years of aloneness in ten exquisite seconds.

I could see nothing there in the dark other than vague hints and outlines. But I imagined I could see the shadow of her smile. That I imagined it was of no consequence. I knew that I had pleased her and that was suddenly the most important thing to me.

As we lay there, sipping the rest of the champagne, giggling out of unsuspected joy, we heard several fire alarms sound in town and in the hills surrounding Riversborough. We didn't pay them much mind, but when a small fleet of fire trucks rolled past the inn, we couldn't help but pause to wonder what the fuss was all about.

"Do you think its the school?" Kira sounded worried.

"I don't think so. The school's in the opposite direction from where those sirens were headed. Do you live on or off campus?"

"That's right," she said, "you don't know where my apartment is."

"Or your phone number."

"If you ask me to marry you again, I might be persuaded to tell you."

"You've already said yes once, I'm not giving you a chance at second thoughts. I've got other means of persuasion." And with those words, I moved quickly to coat my tongue with the taste of her and to fill my head with the scent of jasmine in the snow.

*   *   *

It was still quite dark out when I stirred. After finishing in the bathroom, I was restless with panic and nervous energy. I turned the TV away from the bed and hit the remote's power button. I muted the sound and clicked merrily up and down the channels. On one of the local channels I spotted a graphic of a fire truck. I stopped surfing and turned up the sound ever so slightly:

" . . . fifteen volunteer fire companies, some as far away as Blue Sky Lake, joined Riversborough firefighters in their efforts to bring the blaze under control. As of yet, their efforts have met with little success. Now, for a live update, here's Linda Di Corona at the scene."

Linda Di Corona's audio feed wasn't up and running, but the caption beneath the live picture of her standing in front of a fire truck told me all I needed to know. The ski resort at Cyclone Ridge was burning down. Given the presence of the woman sleeping in my bed, I wasn't about to question the power of coincidence, but a fire at Cyclone Ridge was just too damned convenient. I shut off the TV. I paced for a few minutes, tried reading, surrendered, at last, to fitful sleep.

I don't remember what ring it was when I got to the phone, but I was glad to see Kira was undisturbed from the depths of her dreams.

"Klein?" It was MacClough.

"Who were you expecting, Chancellor Bismarck? Christ, MacClough, it's 2:30 in the morning."

"He can write books and tell time, too. I know what time it is. I just wanted to tell you that I'll be back up there in a few hours and we've got to move fast."

"Why's that?" I was worried. "Did something go sour with Zak?"

"Calm down, Klein. It's just that I've established a definite link between all the parties involved. It seems that Detective Caliparri used to do a little moonlighting as a private investigator for a certain lawyer we both know."

"Jeffrey!"

"None other. I had a chat with Caliparri's widow this afternoon. From what I can piece together, your brother didn't blow off the Valencia Jones case at first blush like everybody seems to think. Back when Zak asked him to take the case, your brother hired Caliparri to have a look. But the case looked like a dog. I mean, she does look guilty as hell and her family tree doesn't help. So Caliparri must've warned Jeffrey off. Then," MacClough stopped to clear his throat, "a few days ago, Caliparri's wife says her husband took another trip up to Riversborough. It was right after your nephew disappeared."

"Shit!"

"We gotta get a look inside those buildings at Cy—"

"Forget it," I cut him off. "They're two steps ahead of us." I began to sing to the tune of "London Bridge": Cyclone Ridge is burning down, burning down, burning down. Cyclone Ridge is burning down, my dear detective."

"Fuck!"

"My feelings exactly."

"You know," he said, "it means we're close, real close. Did you say anything to the girl?"

"The girl's not our problem. That's the good news. I'll tell you all about it when I see you. You want me to pick you up at the airport?"

"No, not worth the risk."

"Listen, John, I know this sounds weird, but I think we should also stop meeting in our rooms. I'm not sure about this, but it could be the desk clerk is our mole."

"Where then?"

I thought about that. It's tough to think of a secure meeting place when you don't know an area all that well.

"Mens room of the Manhattan Court Coffee House. Check there for me every few hours. Coffee's good, poetry sucks, but you'll live."

"Every few hours?" he puzzled. "What are you doin' tomorrow."

"Getting a marriage license." I hung up.

Now I was really wound up. I peered over at Kira. She sort of half smiled at me.

"Is everything all right, Dylan?"

"Sure is," I lied. I kissed the corner of her eye and stroked her hair until she fell back asleep.

I got up and took a shower to occupy some time. A few minutes later, I heard Kira stirring about in the room. I cursed myself for making too much noise, but I figured there was great potential for fun in making it up to her. As I shaved around my beard, I could no longer hear her and figured she'd gone back to sleep. I laughed at my reflection and vowed to make it up to her anyway.

Stepping from the bathroom, I hesitated. There it was again, that feeling someone uninvited was there in the dark. And this time, I was certain. Exposed by the light spilling out of the bathroom, I caught the faint reflection of a man in the mirror hung above the bureau. He was trying to hide himself in the corner and his body *was* partially obscured by shadows and the drapery. But I recognized his face: the desk clerk. My eyes shifted to the bed. Empty!

I pushed the panic down as far as I could, trying to think

of what I might be able to use as a weapon. I figured I could take the guy in the corner, but I got the sense that he didn't have the balls to try a stunt like breaking into my room alone. I was right again. To my left, I could hear a muffled voice, Kira's. I'll always think she was trying to warn me, but I won't ever know. She was gagged or there was a hand covering her mouth. The muffled cries ended abruptly.

Acting as if I'd forgotten something, I took a step back into the bathroom and began to close the door. I wasn't quick enough. The door pushed in on me, knocking me off balance. A strong fist, aimed at my chin, caught me on the point of the shoulder and sent me sprawling on the tile floor. My temple banged into the claw foot of the cast-iron tub. Dazed, I tried standing, but the owner of the strong fist had other ideas.

I caught a glimpse of him just before his left hook introduced itself to my ribs. He was taller than me, about 6'2", blond, and built like a linebacker. Dressed in a shiny lycra suit that highlighted the cut lines between his muscles, he moved effortlessly. I guessed he was the ski dude MacClough said had followed me from the airport. I remember him smiling at me as his knuckles tried their best to make a tunnel through my thorax. It's always a pleasure to see a man who enjoys his work.

I dropped an elbow to block his punch, but I only deflected it to the worst possible spot. It hit right under the center of my rib cage in the solar plexus. My body gave up on the notion of standing. The air couldn't rush out of my lungs fast enough and once out, I couldn't get any back in. I rolled on the tiles trying to force myself to breathe. Somehow, I managed to do that, but I can't tell you how.

Ski dude stopped me from writhing by grabbing me by the throat. That got my attention. At that point, I was pretty well prepared to die. I don't know what made me do what I did next—maybe it was the Brooklyn in me—but I smiled back at him and tried spitting in his face. He didn't like that too well.

Then, seeing I was not much of a threat, the desk clerk stepped into the bathroom. I recall him shaking his head at me and saying: "What an asshole. Okay, it's time for Mr. Sandman."

And it was, too. Lights went out all over the world, just like in *The Day the Earth Stood Still*.

*　　　*　　　*

You know you're fucked when it's hard to tell which part of your body you'd like to have amputated first. I voted for the guillotine; kill the head and the body dies. Why bother doing it piecemeal? When I lifted myself off the tile, the lifting didn't last long. The earth was spinning again. I made it to the sink and buried my head in a basin full of cold water. I can't say that it felt good. I'd say it made things feel less horrible. When I picked my head out of the sink, I saw that the water had turned pinkish. One peek in mirror showed me why. My face was covered in jagged scratches, most not very deep, but some had drawn blood.

Seeing those scratches got me very scared for myself, but mostly for Kira. I could feel the nausea rising in me as I tried lying to myself about what I would find in the bedroom. Kira would be fine, I told myself. They had just taken her as a warning to me to let things go, to give up my search for Zak. Or maybe they had just slapped her around a bit to show me they could get to me. I wasn't a very good liar, especially to myself. I had read too many books using this scenario. Raymond Chandler had used it in a short story before he had even created Philip Marlowe. I had used it in *They Don't Play Stickball in Milwaukee*.

I was rigid, my hands glued to the sink. I could not force myself to look at what I knew I would find in the bedroom. No matter what games I played, no matter the ploy, I could not move. And then, as if on cue, I heard sirens in the distance. Of course, they would play out the scenario all the way. Now, if I wanted to survive, I had no choice but to move.

There would be no wedding. There would be no bride. There would be no drunken party at the Rusty Scupper with MacClough crying in the middle of his toast to me and to my bride. There would be no one to lift us up on chairs as the klezmer band—one that knew some traditional Japanese folk songs—played a hora. There would be no confused in-laws trying to reconcile sushi with pickled herring. There

116

would be no laughter over silly gifts. There would be no kiss at the altar nor broken glasses nor *mazel tovs* nor whatever they say in Japanese for luck. Kira was dead.

I didn't dwell on her. She was gone to someplace better. It was only her body there hanging off the bed headfirst. I knew what the police would find. My skin and blood would be under her fingernails. My semen would be in her vagina. They would comb her pubis and find my hair. She would be bruised, cut maybe, to show there had been a fierce struggle. The cops would find the emptied champagne bottle and probably some planted drugs. I noticed I was crying when I said goodbye.

I ran up to MacClough's room. As I ran, my grief turned to self-loathing. Not only had I managed to get Kira killed, but I had made myself the world's most incredibly stupid and perfect suspect. When the cops began investigating the crime, they would find a pattern of behavior on my part that would suggest stalking. The waitress, Sandra, would claim I had spent the morning questioning her about Kira. She would claim, with a clear conscience, that she had told me about Kira because she was afraid of me and that I had been acting paranoid; something about men trying to follow me. She had taken my bribe only to humor me. The guy in the clothing store would say I had bought a disguise—"You wouldn't recognize your own mother in that outfit with those glasses"—and would say I had acted irrationally about sending the old clothing back to Sound Hill. The woman at the register would say I had acted oddly about her simple request to drink coffee out of a coffee container. Students would come forward to say that they remembered me lingering outside all of Kira's classes that day, some would recall me following her. And as the *piece de resistance*, Prof. Jane Courteau would recount my rather weird story about wanting to use Kira's artwork on my next book. Obviously, I was irrational, obsessed, paranoid. The shrinks would theorize that I had been deeply affected by my recent failure in Hollywood, my father's tragic death, and the disappearance of my beloved nephew:

"Discovering that his nephew had had a previous relationship with the girl, Mr. Klein, due to his precarious mental health, became fixated with Ms. Wantanabe, believing that she was in some way responsible for the disappearance of his nephew. As the fixation turned to obsession, Mr. Klein's paranoid delusions grew in scope and intensity until he became convinced that Ms. Wantanabe was not only responsible for the nephew's disappearance, but had ultimately to suffer the consequences for her actions."

I was nude but for a bloody bath towel. I was unsure why I was running to MacClough's room nor had I any idea of what I'd do when I got there. But MacClough's sense of anticipation was legendary and, like his old buddies used to tell me, Johnny could see trouble coming around the corner before they could see the corner. I knew he wasn't there, but I prayed he had left a spare key tucked away somewhere. I was clutching at straws. Straws, however, seem like fine options when your only other choice is a blood-soaked bath towel.

And when the doorknob turned in my hand, I thought MacClough had proved his legend once again. Under other circumstances I might've entered more cautiously, but cautiously wasn't on the menu this morning. I rushed in without hesitation. The place was a mess, ransacked like Zak's rooms and Caliparri's place. So much for MacClough's anticipation. I threw on any clothes I could find and a pair of John's too-small shoes.

I ran to the end of the hall and climbed down the back fire escape. It was snowing like a son of a bitch and the wind nearly blew me off the bottom ladder. I jumped into a snowdrift. Brushing myself off, I heard sirens blaring around the front of the inn. I thought about making a run for it in my rental, but I couldn't have gotten very far very fast in this kind of storm. I took off on foot under the murky light of dawn. I needed to buy myself a few hours. There were debts that needed paying. I would hide behind the snowflakes if I had to.

The late-season blizzard and the confusion caused by the fire at Cyclone Ridge had worked for me. I had stopped at a pay phone and called for a taxi to pick me up and take me to the airport. Because of the blowing snow, the driver didn't get a good look at my scratched face until after I was in the backseat and we were well on our way. He was a bald man in his mid to late fifties who looked like the only exercise he got involved walking to and from the doughnut shop. He chewed on the unlit butt end of a cigar and kept a yellow pencil tucked behind his right ear. He kind of reminded me of my dad.

I watched his dull brown eyes get wide and shiny in the rearview mirror when he noticed my face. I read his name off his pictured license and pressed my knuckle as hard as I could into the back of his seat.

"You got a wife and kids, Milton?" I asked with icy cool curiosity.

"Two grown kids and three grand kids. Wife's dead."

"Mine too . . . Now."

That got his attention as I had intended it to and he began chomping vigorously on his cigar.

"Listen, Milton," I said, pressing his seat back, "we can do this hard or easy. I've had enough hard for one day. What do you say to easy."

"I like easy."

"Good. Drive me to the border."

I made him give me his coat and the cap he kept on the seat next to him. I took twenty dollars and vowed to get it all back to him, the money with interest. He said that wouldn't be necessary. When we were several miles out of Riversborough, I pulled my fist out of the vinyl seat and pretended to put the phantom gun in my pocket.

"Pull over," I ordered. "I've gotta take a piss."

He really started sweating now and I hated to do it to him, but I was in a tough spot.

"Please, mister, don't ki—"

"Calm down and pull over."

He did as I asked. I got out of the car and walked far enough away to give Milton the confidence he could leave without me being able to catch up or to shoot him. From behind a group of rocks, I watched and waited, hoping he would jump at this chance to escape from the crazed killer I let him think I was. Like any sensible man, he seized the moment. The back end of his old Impala fishtailed like mad on the icy road as he sped off. Now all he had to do was tell the cops I was headed across the border.

It only took me ten minutes to flag down a semi going back toward town. I told the driver my jeep was stuck in a snowbank on an access road about a half mile from where he picked me up. He didn't seem to have any trouble believing it. And between MacClough's turned-up shirt collar and the hood of Milton's coat, I did a good job of hiding my damaged face. Everything was going fine until the trucker moved to turn on the radio.

Maybe I was just the slightest bit tense, but I couldn't help thinking he might reassess his faith in my story if he heard about Kira's murder on the news. One good look at my face and I was finished. Unfortunately, I could not think of single good reason for him not to turn on the radio nor was I in any position to play tough guy with the driver. He had forearms the size of my thighs and a neck like a tree stump. In any case, my plan rested on my ability to get back into Riversborough without attracting attention.

We listened to a few minutes of commercials, one for a Canadian grocery chain. The jingle mixed French and English lyrics. I hummed along, but the sweat had already begun to seep through my shirt. When I noticed that all the ads were for Canadian products, I relaxed some. There was a weather report, a traffic report. I got downright comfortable. Then, there was a news bulletin.

"This again," I spoke loudly enough to drown out the announcer.

"What's that?"

"You didn't hear? There was a big fire up at the Cyclone Ridge ski resort just outside of Riversborough. It took fifteen fire companies to fight it and I don't think even that many got it under control."

"Jesus. Anybody hurt?"

"They didn't say," I answered.

"Probably a little man-made lightning," the driver said, winking at me. "That place's been a white elephant since the new owners spruced it up about five years ago. I don't think they ever got to full bookings in that whole time. Where'd you say you was from?"

The bulletin was over and I didn't like turn the conversation was taking. Besides, we had already entered Riversborough's city limits.

"This is fine," I said, picking a spot arbitrarily. "Thanks. Drive safe."

The air brakes whooshed and the wheels squealed as we came to a stop. I was down and out of the semi's cab before the trucker could question my sanity. I waved bye as he pulled away from the curb. The sun was up, though I couldn't see it through the clouds and blowing snow. I knew about where I was and figured it would take me about an hour of walking through back alleyways to get to where I wanted to go.

*   *   *

There were more customers in the shop than I had suspected would turn out in such awful weather. That unnerved me a bit, but no one had cause to pay me any more mind than the next browser. Mostly everybody in the store still had his or her hood or hat on. I just tried harder than anyone else to stare at my shoes as I searched for the man I had come to see. And when I approached him, there was nothing in his demeanor to indicate that he recognized me. To the casual observer, he treated me as he might've treated any customer coming to enlist his aid.

"I need your help," I said in a voice as flat as Kansas. "I'm looking for the true crime section."

"Come this way, sir."

Rajiv Gupta, the man I was betting my life on was Guppy, led me to a dark corner of the store.

"Here we are, sir. The section is pitifully small, but we don't have strong demand for this sort of thing in

121

Riversborough. Our clientele are mostly students from the college. I'm afraid they tend to be preoccupied with more scholarly works or trendy periodicals."

"I guess I'll have to make due." I knelt down and gestured toward a book I picked out at random. "What do you think of this?"

Kneeling down beside me, he removed the book from the shelf and handed it to me: *Crimes of the Ancient Mariner*. Great! It was the recounting of the gruesome rape-homicides of several young prostitutes by a phony sea captain. It was an unfortunate choice.

"It is not this author's best work," Gupta explained for the benefit of a woman standing only five or six feet away. "We are out of his other book. Let me write the title down for you and maybe you can pick it up at one of the larger chain stores."

He removed a business card from his pocket and began writing furiously on the back of it. He handed it to me, giving me only several seconds to digest what he'd scribbled. There was an address on Oneonta Place, that was clear. He had also written down: "Blue Subaru, broken windshield, Bracken Street, 2 lunchtime." I had barely finished reading when he snapped the card out of my hand and shredded it. He shoved the pieces in his pocket.

"Excuse me," he apologized, "I've gotten my authors confused. That was not the title at all."

The woman in the aisle with us turned and moved into the next row. Gupta pulled his hand back out of his pocket and threw something down that clanged when it hit the floor.

"You've dropped your keys."

"So I did." I retrieved the lifeline he had tossed me. There was a Subaru ignition key on the ring. "Thanks."

"No bother. Should I fetch you the title of that other book?"

"No," I said, "that won't be necessary. I think I've gotten what I need."

"Very good, sir," Gupta bowed slightly and moved on.

I lingered, pretending to study the dust jackets of one or two books. When I thought enough time had passed, I started for the store exit. So close to refuge, I was more nervous now than at any other point during my flight from the law. I could not force myself to focus and I paid for my sloppiness. At the end of the true crime aisle, I stumbled right into the woman who had been standing with Gupta and me during the better part of our charade. Her head hit my cheek.

"Oh, I'm sorry," she apologized, staring directly at my face. "You're cut."

"That's all right, it's nothing."

But even as I rushed by her, I could see that her mind was working overtime to try and explain how a relatively mild impact had caused the scratches on my face. I didn't bother to try and help her thought processes along. What would I have said? "Forgive the scratches, I was attacked by a snow leopard on my way out of the house this morning." I'm afraid not. I simply moved on quickly, forcing myself not to bolt.

Around the corner from the store, I could no longer control the panic and ran for the Subaru. Luckily, there were only four cars parked on Bracken street. The snow had rendered the four unrecognizable. I found Gupta's car on my second guess. I listened to the radio as I drove. I was big news in the little town and my worst fears had been confirmed. Having discovered copious amounts of tissue, blood, and some clipped hairs under the victim's fingernails, the police were postulating that my face had been scratched deeply. Now I had to find Oneonta Place before the woman in the book store found the knob to her car radio. Although it was probably my best bet of finding Gupta's house in a hurry, I didn't think stopping to ask directions was a terribly prudent idea.

Buddy Holly

There *were* unattractive areas in Riversborough, Oneonta Place was proof of that. It was an ugly street even under a frosting of virgin snow. Snow couldn't hide the boarded windows on every other L-shaped ranch. Snow could not hide the for-sale signs, the foreclosure notices posted on the lawns. Decay has a nasty habit of defeating the best camouflage.

Number 74 Oneonta Place was unremarkable as seen from the street. Half the slats were missing from the picket fence that surrounded the lot. The house itself was a faded gray, but it had been patched in various spots with asbestos shingles that neither matched one another nor the shingles that covered the remainder of the ranch. There were two headless lawn jockeys, half buried in snow, holding plaster lanterns on either side of the pink front door.

I pushed the button on the remote garage door opener as I pulled into the driveway and, much to my surprise, the thing actually worked. The light in the garage stayed on as the door closed behind the old Subaru. I could breathe again. The light popped off, but I stood there in the semidarkness for quite a while. Soaked with sweat, my body shaking beyond my control, I thought of Kira, the woman, not the victim, for the first time since I'd run from my room. It didn't take any courage to cry now.

I entered the house through a door in the garage. The house was neater than I would have expected. The furnishings and carpeting were old, but clean and dusted. All the shades were drawn, so I could move about freely without having to crawl by windows and doors. There was an eat-in kitchen, a big living room, and three bedrooms with one full bath at the end of a long hall. Only the smallest of the three bedrooms seemed to function as a bedroom. The middle-sized bedroom was set up as an office. There was a writing desk with an IBM Selectric typewriter on it, diplomas on the walls—a B.S. from Cornell, a Masters degree from MIT. There was no Ph.D., but there was a rectangular spot on the wall where another diploma might once have hung—a three-year-old calendar and an oil portrait of a breathtakingly exotic woman in traditional Indian dress. The gold accents and the vibrant reds and blues in her clothing flowed in stark contrast to her deep brown skin and pitch black hair. Her lips were simultaneously shy and inviting. And the artist had given the dark beauty a sense of motion I could not accurately describe. I could not say that her hair blew in a painted breeze. I could not say that her eyes followed me or that her mouth smiled when I turned my head a certain way. It just seemed so to me.

What would have been the master bedroom served as a storage area and library. If he had read half the books in the room, he had read twice as many as I had. Apparently, he also spoke several languages. But what I liked best was that he owned both the English hardcover and Chinese paperback editions of *Coney Island Burning* and *They Don't Play Stickball in Milwaukee*. It took the translators quite some time to convert the Yiddish slang into proper Mandarin.

So, I thought as I turned out of the doorway, with the exception of the woman's portrait, the interior of Guppy's house was as unremarkable as the exterior. Then it struck me that there was no computer in sight, not even a word processor. And I felt confident Guppy hadn't built his legend on an old IBM Selectric. I didn't like it, not at all. I ran to find the stairs to the basement.

No sign of a computer there, just a line of bare bulbs with pull chains and the oil burner. There was a washer and dryer, a slop sink and a small shop. My head filled with maybes. Maybe Guppy's myth was just that, myth. Maybe he used a laptop, a notebook. Maybe he rented an office someplace. Maybe he used someone else's equipment. Maybe I was being set up like Humpty Dumpty to take a great fall. Maybe, maybe, maybe . . .

What I liked even less than the computer whiz with no computer that was down in his basement I was getting that same eerie sensation I had had twice in my hotel room, only stronger this time. There was somebody else here or there just had been. I wouldn't have been at all surprised to turn a corner and find a lit cigarette burning in an ashtray. But there were no corners I hadn't turned. The closets upstairs were mostly filled with air and there wasn't any spot in the cellar I couldn't see well from where I was standing. Like I said before, alcohol didn't work for me, but I needed a drink.

I stripped down, threw my collection of other folks' sweaty clothes in the wash, and went upstairs to shower. I stopped at the fridge—stocked better than any single man's refrigerator I had ever seen—and grabbed a bottle of Brighton Beach Brown Ale. I froze in my tracks. Brighton Beach Brown Ale, or Triple B as its devotees called it, was a gourmet microbrewed beer from Brooklyn. It wasn't widely distributed even in the New York City area. How did Rajiv Gupta come to have a six-pack, I wondered? It was as if I had been expected. This feeling like I was caught in the middle of a *Twilight Zone* episode was getting pretty tiresome, but I was nude and confused and had nowhere else to turn. I drank the Triple B in two gulps and took a shower that used up all the hot water the washing machine could spare.

*   *   *

I stepped out of the shower. I grabbed for the towel I knew I had left atop the hamper, but it was not there. The steam, thicker than London fog, conspired with the bright bathroom light to blind me. I would not have been able to see my own reflection in the mirror. I could not find the mirror nor could I find the hand I held up before my face. I did not panic. I pressed my palms to the wet tile and felt for the door. It was a tiny bathroom, not much bigger than an old-fashioned phone booth, but the walls were seamless and had swallowed the door whole. I dropped to my knees to feel the floor. The floor was mud and grass. I could see and smell down here. The root ends of tulips—I don't know how I knew they were tulips—stuck up in the air. The fine root hairs waved in a wind that blew only close to the ground.

I put my face to the earth and stretched out, my legs seeming to extend into infinity. I closed my eyes and prayed to sleep. My feet flapped in the wind like the points of pennants. I was warm from the inside out, but only for a moment. The tulip roots grew around my limbs, pulling me

126

down into the earth. I could not breathe. I tried to move, but was frozen. Somehow, my left arm was free and I latched my hand onto the bathroom sink. Pulling myself up, I noticed I was floating. I willed myself to come down. My feet landed on cold tile.

Though the steam was still thick, it was cold on my skin like a marble shroud. I could see the mirror and myself in it, covered in mud. Someone was there with me in the cold steam. It was a woman. The scent of her raw patchouli filled up my senses, but I could not see her. I felt her hands surround me, spin me, stroke me. I was faint. I felt her lips pressed to mine. I heard the rustle of fabric. I opened my eyes and she was there; the woman in the portrait. Her tongue tasted of honey and fire. Her hard nipples pressed through her sari into my flesh. We spun as we kissed, faster and faster. I was dizzy with her scent, her kisses, the spinning. She bit into my tongue and the spinning stopped.

I heard her laughing from very far away. A hand pushed me through the shower curtain and I fell through the bottom of the earth. I did not fall through air. I could breathe well enough, but it was like falling through black tar that restricted me without adhering to me. A door opened somewhere in the universe and the tar let go. The ground rushed up to greet me. I landed so hard the air exploded out of me. I felt skin beneath me. Kira's body had broken my fall. Her dead eyes looked up, accusing me. An icy cold hand shook my shoulder. I rolled over.

"Mr. Klein. Mr. Klein, are you quite all right?"

I was looking up from the living room floor at Rajiv Gupta, his coat sprinkled with snow.

"I'm not sure what all right means anymore," I said, picking myself up.

"You were dreaming?"

"That was no dream."

"No," he agreed, "in your circumstance, I don't imagine dreaming is what a man does in his sleep."

"What time is it?"

He looked at his wrist. "Two twenty-seven in the afternoon."

"Lunchtime. " I wiped the sleep from my eyes.

"Normally, yes, but because of the weather, I am finished for the day."

I put my right hand out. "Thanks for saving me. Maybe we can talk about why you did it a little later."

"We can do that." He shook my hand. "Are you hungry?"

"For answers."

"You and the police. That woman at the end of the aisle heard a news report on you when she arrived back at her flat."

"I was afraid of that," I confessed. "Were they rough on you?"

"Not at all." He laughed. "I played the frightened immigrant, waving my hands and praising God. I've perfected it over the years. It's gotten me out of a number of fixes. That day I met you in the coffee house, I was doing a variation on the theme. The wise Eastern philosopher, full of vague platitudes for anyone who will listen."

"Who is the woman in the portrait?"

"Has she gotten under your skin already?" He smirked, then remembering the scratches on my face and the reason for my being here, he apologized. "That was unforgivable."

"Forget it. Who is she?"

"No one, really. An ideal woman. She has come to me in my dreams for years. In exchange for some help I gave a friend, she painted that portrait from my description. It is quite good, that painting."

I agreed. "Amazing."

"I know she exists somewhere," Guppy explained, tapping his heart. "She may look nothing like the portrait, but I will recognize her spirit."

"I believe you will. So . . ."

"So?" he puzzled.

"Where's the computer? And please, don't wave your hands around and praise God. I don't give up so easy as the Riversborough Police."

"You do have questions."

"I'm just getting warmed up," I said. "How is it you just happen to have Triple B in the fridge? And what is it you know about Zak you weren't telling me that day at the coffee house? And how in the hell do you know I didn't kill the girl?"

"Come, Mr. Klein, let me unburden your heart. The questions will answer themselves."

I was getting a little tired of Guppy the wise philosopher and I would have appreciated a straight answer. Instead, I followed him down to the basement. We went into his little workshop. There was a workbench with some hand tools. There were shelves with rows of baby food jars used to store screws and nails and nuts and bolts. Unlike the furnishings upstairs, the shop was a bit dusty. Suddenly it occurred to me that this was the one place in the house that seemed not to fit. The furniture upstairs certainly wasn't new, but it was modern, more or less. The tools on the workbench were wooden-handled, from another era. Even the baby jars seemed dated. I picked one up. The lid was the old-fashioned kind from when I was a kid, the type you had to pry off with a special tool.

"From the original owner," Guppy said, sensing my curiosity. "And so is this."

He reached down to the floor and unhinged some latches hidden behind the legs of the workbench. He stood and repeated the process with some other latches hidden in a storage cabinet. If you didn't know they were there, you would never have noticed those latches. I got the feeling that that was the whole idea. Guppy tugged at one end of the workbench and it pulled off the wall quite easily. He pulled away a strip of old yellow insulation to expose what looked like a bulkhead door from a WWII submarine.

"If it's not a U-boat," I said, "it must be a bomb shelter."

"Very good, Mr. Klein. A bomb shelter it is."

Guppy unscrewed the heavy steel wheel, releasing the thick pins which sealed the door against nuclear attack. There was an audible gush of air as the seal was broken. He yanked the door open and stepped in before me, flicking on a light switch. He asked me to come in, but to wait as he pulled the workbench roughly back into place. When he had done so, he pulled the bulkhead door closed and spun the handle shut.

We were on a short flight of metal stairs surrounded by

bare concrete. The concrete was probably a good foot or two thick. The light fixture was a simple steel cage fixed over a lightbulb. At the bottom of the stairs was another bulkhead door, only this one was more of a hatch than a door. Again, Guppy spun the heavy wheel to release the seal. Almost immediately, I could hear music coming from inside the shelter. I recognized the song, but not the band. It was a techno-pop version of the old Buddy Holly song, "Maybe Baby." Guppy opened the hatch and pointed to a bar above it.

"Feet first," he instructed as I grabbed the bar. "And, Mr. Klein, try to remember what desperation feels like to you."

Some more vague advice to be shrugged off. I climbed through the open hatch. The music was louder now, but the room was black. Beneath the bassline of the music, I thought I could hear someone snoring. Guppy bumped into me as he came into the shelter. He apologized and before turning on the lights, said: "What we did, we did to save an innocent person. Our intentions were pure. You have to believe that. We could not foresee what would happen to the girl."

"Look, I appreciate what you've done for me, but I'm really starting to lose my patience. Now what the fuck are you talking about?"

But Guppy did not have to answer. He did not even have to turn on the light. Because out of the blackness came the voice that would make it all clear to me.

"Hey, Uncle Dylan, is that you?"

Fairness

The lights came up, and, just for a moment, so did my heart.

Zak jumped down from the upper cot of two that folded off the wall. He kissed me, threw his big arms around me and bear-hugged me for a long few seconds. But my joy in discovering him alive had already gone out of me. I was stiff and numb in his grasp. He backed off, searching for clues in the lines and scratches in my face. Guppy stood silently behind me. The synthesized music droned on as Buddy Holly spun in his grave.

I turned to Guppy: "Fuck good intentions! Your road to hell is paved with innocent bodies."

"He doesn't know about her, Mr. Klein."

"Who don't I know about?" Zak was impatient.

"The girl who dug her nails into my face after she'd been strangled. Will you please shut that fucking music off?"

Guppy came around between Zak and me and flicked off the clock radio, which sat on a small shelf amidst the most impressive and relatively compact computer workstation I'd ever seen in a noncommercial setting.

"Who don't I know about?" Zak repeated.

"Please," Gupta implored, "give us a chance to explain."

"Explain!" I was screaming. "You want to explain? Here, schmuck, let's go find a phone. Either one of you two fluent in Japanese?"

Zak shrank back. "Japanese!"

"That's right, Zak, Kira's dead, thanks to you two clowns. You get on the phone and explain it to her father, because I couldn't give a shit about what either of you has to say. If you want to play God, become a writer. Otherwise, omnipotence is best left in the hands of puppeteers and lunatics."

Zak was crying.

Guppy fought back: "We were trying to save—"

"—Valencia Jones. I know that," I said. "You've traded Kira's life for hers. I sure as shit hope she's worth it."

"She's innocent," Zak yelled. "She's innocent!"

"Maybe she is, but she's still on trial and I'm next. How

could you jerk everybody around like this? You missed Grandpa's funeral. Your whole family is sick. For chrissakes, Zak, they think you're dead! *I* thought you were dead!"

"I didn't know how else to get anyone's attention," Zak said sheepishly. "Valencia was going to jail for a long time and no one would listen."

"Oh, you got peoples' attention, all right. Your father hired a Castle-on-Hudson detective to look into Valencia's case. I figure his funeral was probably yesterday. Then there's this guy, Steven Markum, he worked up at Cyclone Ridge. He was probably the guy that planted the Isotope in Valencia Jones' car. He conveniently broke his neck skiing the other day. Cyclone Ridge is burning down as we speak. Your dorm room and room at home were both ransacked. The best friendship I ever had is probably over. I'm wanted for murder. And let's not forget to throw Kira's body on top of the pile like a cherry on top of a sundae. Yeah, Zak, I'd say you got people to listen."

"That's not fair, Uncle Dylan."

"No," Gupta chimed, "it is not."

"Welcome to life on earth, fellas. What's fairness got to do with anything?"

"When I was a kid," Zak said, "I thought fairness meant everything to you. I looked up to you because of that, because you were so different from my dad. Money didn't matter to you. What was right mattered."

"Money's easy not to care about when you haven't got any. Fairness and what's right don't even count in horseshoes."

"I can't believe I'm hearing this from you, Uncle Dylan. Uncle Josh used to tell me stories about you."

"What stories?"

"About you in the old neighborhood and how the other kids respected you for doing the right thing all the time. Even my dad admires you for how you used to stick up for Larry Feld and his family."

"Your dad hates Larry Feld and thought his family was crazy. And as for my brother Josh, he was the one who bestowed upon me the title of family fuck-up."

"Well, I guess I'm no longer a pretender to the throne, am I, Uncle Dylan? I really am the family fuck-up now."

That punch got through and it hurt like a son of a bitch. I knew Zak and Guppy hadn't meant for anyone to get hurt, certainly not killed. Hadn't I done an incredible amount of impulsive things and used love and desperation as justifications? But people had been killed and there was no escaping the bloody trail that led to my nephew's hideaway.

"Okay," I said. "If we're going to keep Valencia Jones' ass out of prison and mine off death row, we better get to work figuring out just how. We can save the recriminations for our next family meal. Agreed?"

They were glad to sign on for that. I told Guppy to get his coat back on, he was going to meet an ex-cop in the mens room of the Manhattan Court Coffee House.

"What if Mr. MacClough should be suspicious of me?"

"He already is . . ." I hesitated. "What should I call you, anyway?"

"Raj, Rajiv, Guppy... What you call me is of no significance, Mr. Klein. I will know you are speaking to me."

"Jesus, how did I know I'd get an answer like that? Like I was saying, MacClough is already suspicious and when he hears about Kira's murder, he's gonna be very tense about being approached by a stranger. Just tell him that I hate brandy, even Izzy Three Legs Weinstein's. He'll understand."

Reimbursement

We sat there together for what seemed hours, not talking, avoiding each other's eyes. I cleaned lint that wasn't there, checked a watch I wasn't wearing, looked for dirt under my clean nails. It was the first awkward time in our lives as uncle and nephew. We had always been a team, Zak and me, two men cut from the same pattern. There had never been any attempt to deny it. The poor kid really did look and sound like me, though Zak lacked the Brooklyn patois. He further lacked some of his uncle's hard edges and street smarts. Before today, I had felt that was to his advantage. He was less suspicious, could see the sun sometimes behind the clouds.

I remembered when I was living back in Brooklyn, working my first insurance jobs for Larry Feld. I let Zak— he was only a little guy back then, three or four—tag along with me for the day. But it was safe and easy work that Saturday. All we had to do was take a few Polaroids of cracked sidewalks and dangerous intersections for Larry. We were on Kings Highway when Zak got hungry and told me he had to go *winkies*. Walking back to my car when we were done eating, Zak tugged my hand and asked me: "Why are you doing that, Uncle Dylan?"

"What am I doing, Zak?"

"Why do you slow down all the time and look at your face in the store windows?"

He was exactly right. I did stop and stare, but I had never given much thought to the reasons why.

"I don't know," I recall saying. "I guess I slow down to let the people pass. I don't think I like it when people get too close behind me."

He looked at his hand in mine and then up at me. "It's okay for me to be close, Uncle Dylan?"

"You? Always, kiddo. Always."

Sure, it was cute, but that's not why it had stuck with me all these years. On that day I realized Zak had the power to make me look at myself in ways and at times I would have never thought to look. He was like a part of me that could step outside myself and hold a mirror up to the dark places I avoided. And now he was doing it again, holding up the dark mirror.

"You expected me to come," I spoke to Zak, "didn't you?"

"Hoped, Uncle Dylan, not expected."

"But you had my favorite beer in the fridge."

"My favorite, too." He hesitated, then asked: "Are you still mad at me?"

"I'm still mad at everyone, from your father to my agent, from Grandpa to MacClough. I was born mad, you know that. You weren't, Zak. It's one of the really good parts about the differences between us."

"I get mad, really mad."

"There's a big difference between getting and being," I said, "a big fucking difference."

"I guess."

"Go upstairs and get us a couple of our favorite beers. When you come back, I think there's some stuff we need to explain to each other."

He went first. He told me about Kira and their brief affair and how they agreed they were better off as friends. Zak's recap of his first meeting with Valencia Jones was right in line with what she had said. Zak was self-aware. He knew he was a sucker for sadness and Valencia Jones had sadness to spare. And though Riversborough College was allegedly a bastion not only of liberal arts but of liberal thinking, Valencia Jones was almost an immediate outcast. She was black, unspectacular to look at, and as soon as word of her parentage spread through the campus, she was designated a persona non grata.

That was all my nephew needed to know. Zak didn't fall in love with Valencia Jones so much as adopt her cause. Oh, they liked each other well enough, fought through the awkwardness of sexual inexperience together, and went to the movies a lot. Zak was her defender, her confidant. Having met her, I got the feeling she rather needed the confidant more than the defender. Their relationship began to unravel when many relationships do; they were getting bored. You can only play sir knight and damsel in distress for just so long before it gets a wee bit tedious. It was Zak's idea for them to move in together. Stepping back and letting go was not something the Kleins—all the Kleins—did with any ease. Valencia Jones had balked at first, but gave into the idea out of a sense of obligation. Even Zak could see how he had set them up for a big fall.

Just before the Spring break, Valencia Jones begged out of the arrangement. Although he fought it, in true Klein tradition, Zak agreed to the split.

"It was my fault, Uncle Dylan."

"It's been my experience that it takes two to make or break a relationship."

"But that's not what I mean," he barked. "I was the reason she got arrested. I arranged for her to go to Cyclone Ridge."

I choked on that. "I don't understand."

"I was feeling shitty for the way things had gone with us living together. Val really needed to get away from me. I knew that. She was going to go down to Daytona with the rest of the college-aged world, but I talked her into finally trying skiing. She always said she wanted to try it and I had promised to take her sometime. We just never got around to doing it. So I called up there and made a reservation for her. The students at the school get a special discount. You can check, I even paid for it with my dad's credit card."

"Funny how your dad managed to forget to tell me this. Funny how he forgets to mention a lot of things."

"It's the way he controls people," Zak said.

"Tell me about it. He was my big brother a long time before he was your father. So, you feel guilty because you arranged for Valencia Jones' ski weekend. It's wrongheaded thinking, Zak. How could you have known what would happen? It's not like a drug bust was part of the discount package."

"That's cold comfort coming from you and pretty inconsistent. I'm either responsible or not responsible for my inability to foresee future consequences, but not both."

"Consistency is the hobgoblin of little minds, Zak. But you're talking tennis rackets and stickball bats here," I chided. "When you made Valencia's ski reservations, it was an innocent gesture. It would have been unreasonable to suspect anything more ominous than a broken leg to come of it. But there was nothing innocent in your dropping out of circulation. You intended for things to happen, you hoped for it. That's manipulation. It's the difference between the sun and a hydrogen bomb. Some chain reactions are natural and beyond our control, some are purposeful and man-made."

Zak was stunned, absolutely silent, pained. Almost imperceptibly at first, his bottom lip quivered. Large tears poured over his cheeks. He did not bother to wipe them away. I think he literally wanted them to stain his face, to brand him a fool. But he did remain silent.

"I need to be alone right now, Uncle Dylan," he finally spoke and let himself out of the shelter.

The symbolism of his exit was not lost on me. Sometimes the cost of our life lessons comes at our own expense. Sometimes other people have to pay. When they pay with their lives, reimbursement becomes problematical.

Smoke

I didn't have the strength in me not to be happy to see John Francis MacClough. At that moment, I would have forgiven him more than murder. For John had always been magic for me. Though I couldn't swim a stroke, I felt as if I was never in above my head with him about. I guess it was a silly attitude for a man of forty years to have. I realize the irrationality of it, but when he stuck his head through the shelter hatch, I felt as if I would be saved. Alas, my euphoria at the sight of him was short-lived, as his first words to me were: "You're fucked, Klein."

Even that could not ruin my mood entirely. MacClough had been a sort of ploughman's guardian angel, the adopted older brother who could fulfill the promises my blood brothers could not. I had, in some unarticulated way, come to think of Johnny as the brother without the feet of clay. It wouldn't be the first time I'd been wrong.

"Thanks, you shanty Irish prick," I shouted, standing up to hug him. "I'm so fucked, I'm even happy to see your ugly puss."

But when he stepped back from my embrace, his face was blank. Not cold, exactly, just blank. "You're happy even though you think I'm a murderer?"

"The rest of the world thinks I'm one. I guess I got religion all of a sudden. Did the news reach home yet?"

"Not before I left, but I'd say the picture from your investigator's license is probably hitting the airwaves all over North America about now. I'll give you the benefit of the doubt and assume it wasn't you that whacked the whore. Who did it?"

"She wasn't a whore, MacClough. She was my fiancée."

"Maybe we better back up."

I agreed. "Maybe we better."

Johnny sat down on the lower cot and listened carefully to what I had to say. He showed emotion only once, wincing at my description of Kira's body—inert, nude, battered—hanging off the bed. It wasn't the description of her body per se that pained him. I knew that. As a beat cop he'd seen human remains in all manner of horrific states. He used to say he'd found bodies that would make Jack the Ripper's butcher puke. It was the loss at the chance for love that hurt him. Having let the one true love in his life slip through his fingers decades ago, he could not abide the loss of love. Sometimes, I thought, it was MacClough, not me, who possessed the soul of a writer. As an Irishman, he was born with it.

"Who did it, Klein?" he asked, turning away. "Who killed her?"

"It was either the desk clerk or the ski dude or both. I was thankfully unconscious at the time. What am I going to do, John?"

He didn't answer and before I could push him for a response, Guppy came through the hatch with some beers in tow. MacClough said he preferred whiskey, but Guppy had none. He did not believe in alcohol. It clouded the mind, weakened concentration. The only reason he had beer was to appease Zak. It wasn't a religious issue with him.

Finally, after Guppy had explained himself to death, MacClough begged for him to shut up and wondered if Gupta had ever met an indirect answer he didn't like?

"No," was all he said.

When the beers were finished, I bit my lip and asked Guppy to help us understand exactly what he and Zak were up to. It was all well and good, I said, that Zak disappeared, but what significance could that possibly have to a drug distribution ring. Why would a college kid's dropping out of sight lead to three deaths and the destruction of a ski resort? Possibly out of fear of another long-winded explanation, MacClough spoke up.

"Zak knows something and the drug dealers know he knows. What's more, Zak's got proof of what he knows. That's what they were looking for when they tore up Zak's rooms and Caliparri's house."

Guppy's face brightened: "That is essentially correct, but there is solidity at the center of your conclusions. At the center of our plan is smoke and void."

So much for direct answers. MacClough and I found dread in each other's eyes, but neither of us could see our way around asking the question.

"Can you run that by us in something akin to English," I pleaded. Gupta pointed at MacClough. "Mr. MacClough—"

"John," he interrupted. "It's shorter."

"Very well, John. John said that Zak knew something and that the drug dealers knew he knew. Furthermore, he said that Zak could obviously back up with physical proof these things he knew. But the truth is that Zak and myself know nothing about these drug operations. We only have guesses and we could no sooner prove any of those guesses than I could prove that this chair is what it seems."

"What?" MacClough was agitated. "Klein, you're fucked worse than I thought."

"Perception," I told John, "is everything. Perception is reality."

"What have you two been smokin'? You sound like a couple of escapees from a bad philosophers convention."

"Zak knows nothing," Guppy said while laughing at John's bad philosophers comment. "And I know even less. But through a certain dexterity with computers and a carefully planned timetable, Zak and I have been able—"

"—to leave a certain impression." MacClough was catching on. "You mean you guys really don't know anything."

"Nothing. We only know that what we have done is working. The fire at Cyclone Ridge, the break-ins, the murders, and the attempt to frame Mr. Klein tell us that. We have stirred up the beehive, but we have only felt their sting. What we need to know is the bees themselves."

"How'd you manage it?" I wondered.

Guppy sat down at the computer, got his system quickly up and running. His lithe brown fingers fairly glided along the keyboard, hesitating only briefly to afford him the opportunity to scan the monitor. Apparently satisfied, he turned his attention back to MacClough and myself.

"Do you know the Internet, gentlemen?"

We both nodded our heads that we did, but both Johnny and I were quick to point out that we knew very few of the details. MacClough didn't even own a typewriter. Christ, he still used a rotary phone. And I pounded out my work on a temperamental Smith Corona word-processor. Neither of us had the hi-tech sensibility of a Generation X-er.

Guppy correctly figured this meant we didn't know shit about the Internet. He therefore gave us a brief rundown on web sites, chat rooms, and the like. It all seemed pretty detached and dehumanizing to me. MacClough was less put off, but failed to see the point.

"The point, John," Guppy said, "is that you can pick any subject, not nearly any subject, but any subject and you will find someone, maybe thousands of people on-line interested in the same subject. Pick a subject."

"Men who have sex with barnyard animals," MacClough blurted out.

"And the women who love them," I added.

Guppy was too busy massaging the keyboard to laugh. "There. Please, watch the screen."

As he scrolled the list of alternative sex discussion groups by us, John and I stared in amazement at the seemingly endless variations. And while scanning the section on barnyard animals, Guppy stopped the scroll and pointed out a particular group.

"There, Mr. Klein, are the women who love them. Would you like to go into a chat room?"

"So," I interrupted, "what's the point? What's any of this got to do with the price of potatoes in Yemen?"

"Isotope, Klein," MacClough answered.

"Exactly, John," Guppy praised. "Though not so many as alternative sex groups, there are many many drug-related sites on the Internet. And out of these, many deal exclusively with Isotope. And what is the one tangible fact Zak and I had to work with?"

"That Valencia Jones was arrested for carrying a very large quantity of Isotope."

"Exactly, Mr. Klein, exactly. And because the quantity was so huge, Zak and I assumed the people who had planted these hallucinogenics in Miss Valencia's car were not, I believe the phrase is, nickel-and-dime dealers. In these times, smart business people, sophisticated business people—criminal or legitimate—are heavily tapped into the worldwide net. Careful monitoring of the Internet is crucial for the success of any enterprise which services people thirty years of age and under."

"You set them up," MacClough interjected. "I don't know how you did it, but you set them up. You knew they'd be watching."

"We hoped so," Guppy aped Zak's earlier sentiment. "And now we know they were."

Over nearly a tenth-month span, Guppy and Zak had spent several hours a day, seven days a week, leaving cryptic messages in every drug-related chat room on the Internet. The early messages were fairly brief, meant simply to attract attention:

> We know. Love Valencia.

And they would repeat the messages over and over again, whenever they had the opportunity to interact. Gradually, they had expanded the length and the depth of their messages:

> We know the truth. Love Valencia. P.S. You pay one way or the other. Have figured out your system. Love Valencia. Have downloaded. Have disc. You will pay either way.

> Clock is ticking. Tick . . .Tick . . .Tick. Paying me is the trick. Love Valencia. Will testify to sink your ship. Will need six figures to seal my lips.

They carried on like this, never knowing whether anyone was there to listen. But since Jeffrey had turned the case down and Zak saw no other alternative to taking things into his own hands, he and Guppy kept it up. Then, as the trial date approached, they went on the offensive, hinting as to their identity:

> You will see I am real when myself I will conceal. Love Valencia. When a Riversborough student disappears you will know your greatest fears. Remember, ships and lips and figures times six.

Zak and Guppy had an accomplice that we hadn't figured on: Valencia Jones' lawyer. To protect her client, the lawyer had even kept her complicity a secret from Valencia Jones. That explained the lawyer's absence when MacClough and I went to see Valencia Jones in the Mohawkskill jail. But her most important contribution to Zak and Guppy's plan was to add Zak's name to the defense witness list the day after he was reported missing. Only then, after revealing himself, could Zak know if anyone had been reading their messages.

They were unfortunately underwhelmed by the response; there wasn't any. But having never truly entertained the possibility of failure, they had painted themselves into a rather precarious corner. Zak and Guppy had no way of knowing whether their months of messages had gone unread by the people for whom they were intended. That prospect was difficult enough to swallow and meant Valencia Jones was as good as convicted. There was, however, a second possibility, a possibility far more bone-chilling. It dawned upon them that their messages might very well have been received, but that their adversaries were simply lying in wait. After all, now the Isotope dealers knew Zak's identity, but Zak and Guppy were still fumbling around in the dark, tilting at shadows without faces.

That's where their plan had gone awry. They had hoped to somehow set up a meeting with the dealers and alert the police. But when there was no immediate response to Zak's name mysteriously showing up on the witness list, they supposed they were dead in the water. Zak, his life now possibly in danger, thinking his bluff had been called, had no reasonable choice but to remain in hiding until the completion of Valencia Jones' trial. Brave and resourceful as he and Guppy were, they failed to see the value in Valencia Jones' conviction and getting themselves killed.

Instead of completely giving up the ship, they continued to fill up the Isotope chat rooms with their messages:

> Revealed and still concealed. Love Valencia. Don't be shy, I won't be. I'll bring your house down, you will see.

You've called my bluff. You think I am not tough.
Love Valencia. Six figures is no longer enough.

Think I'm scared, we shall see. That disc is what's
important, silly, not me. Tick . . .Tick . . .Tick.

Still nothing. Then Zak remembered a weird thing from
a trial he'd seen on TV. Evidence for possible future use was
handed to the court in a sealed envelope. It wasn't actually
entered into evidence, but was kept by the court for later
introduction. Whether the evidence was admissible or not
would be argued if and when the envelope was unsealed and
its contents offered to the court. The next day, Valencia
Jones' lawyer delivered a sealed brown envelope into the
trial judge's hands. That night Zak and Guppy put out the
following message:

Going once. Going twice. No more playing nice. Love
Valencia. Disc in envelope is a fake. Mine is real.
Make no mistake and make the deal. The clock stops
ticking soon.

It worked, though Zak and Guppy didn't know it, not
right away. On the night they sent that message, Detective
Caliparri left Riversborough for the second and final time.
His visit hadn't gone unnoticed. Although his visit had been
basically innocent and completely fruitless, the Isotope dealers remembered Caliparri's first visit and his nosing around
about Valencia Jones on behalf of Jeffrey Klein. Much to
Caliparri's eventual detriment, the dealers had put two and
two together and come up with five. Apparently, they had
found the timing of Zak's message about the disc, the delivery of the mystery envelope to the judge, and Caliparri's
brief return to Riversborough too great a coincidence to dismiss. Somehow, they had gotten the misguided notion that
Zak had passed the real evidence—which, of course, was not
real at all—on to Caliparri for safekeeping. And when
Caliparri could not produce the disc, he was whacked for his
trouble.

"You see, gentlemen," Guppy said, "once the detective was killed, there could be no turning back. We knew then that they had been reading our messages all along. What we hadn't counted on was murder."

"What did you think they were going to do if you ever had a meeting," I sneered, "kiss you on the lips?"

"We hadn't thought things out that far."

"They would've tortured the truth out of the one of you they got and killed the pair of ya," MacClough shook his head disapprovingly. "You two guys were real smart about this plan. I mean that. But this ain't the kinda game with rules and it's been my experience that civilians don't fare well against killers in those games. And just in case you haven't been keeping score lately, it's them that got us by the balls. Remember, my old pal here," he slapped my shoulder, "is facing the hangman's needle."

"The hangman's needle?" I was incredulous. "The soul of a writer and the syntax of a refugee."

"There's nothing wrong with my syntax that bringing back the electric chair wouldn't fix."

"I don't understand," Guppy seemed perplexed, "truly. How do they have us by the balls?"

"Because the manhunt and the murder charge against Klein are real," MacClough said, "but the evidence and testimony we have to bargain with are phony as a three-dollar bill. There are limitations to what you can do with smoke and void."

Guppy, suddenly looking quite ashen, stood and excused himself. He mentioned needing some time to meditate before talking to Zak. Like Zak before him, it had dawned on Guppy that play time was over, but that killing time might have just begun.

Abraham Lincoln

I don't know how Zak had made it through his weeks of seclusion. I was three days into my life in the bunker and I was ready to turn myself in. MacClough was dealing with it better than me, but he wasn't the current poster boy for *America's Most Wanted*. Ma Barker and Pretty Boy Floyd had nothing on me.

I don't know, I just couldn't get a handle on which part of the ordeal was worst. At times, the fear of capture made me nauseous. Then, minutes later, the world would turn on me and capture would seem like salvation. The apparent hopelessness was getting to me; Existentialism 101. Somewhere, Sartre and Camus were laughing at me. I wondered if the point was to try and evade capture long enough to rate a movie of the week or could I hold on until I inspired an entire series? Alas, no. Quinn Martin was dead.

I hated being scared all the time and I was scared all the time now. Having been scared my whole life, you would've thought I'd've been prepared. I wasn't. This kind of scared was different. This kind of scared was amorphous and specific all at once. But being so scared helped me block out the thoughts of Kira.

In the end, though, it wasn't the insecurity nor the hopelessness nor the fear. It wasn't Guppy's god-awful cooking nor was it speculations over how much Kira had suffered. The worst part, I guess, was knowing that people thought I was a monster. It was eating me whole, inside out. I tried to recall how many times I had recited the cliché: "It doesn't matter what people think of you." It matters, believe me, it matters. I think I understood how MacClough must have hurt when I confronted him about Hernandez's death.

Things were bad for me, but they had just gotten worse for Valencia Jones. The newspapers reported that her trial was back on and that each of her attorney's motions had been denied, most without comment. At least I had the myth of freedom to cling to. Guppy and Zak were bummed to the max and were busy trying to devise some new message to draw their enemies out. I had my own ideas about that, but kept them to myself.

"Guppy," I tugged at his sleeve. "Can I talk to you a minute?"

"Certainly." He followed me out of the shelter into the basement.

"I need to make two phone calls in private. Unfortunately, there's a chance at least one of the lines I'm calling could be tapped. Is there—"

"Yes, Mr. Klein, there is a secure method. Let us say that I have managed to gain access to certain phone systems in other countries which will allow me to route your calls through so many places that the place of origin will be impossible to detect."

"You're sure?" I was skeptical. "I don't want any more innocent people hurt."

"No one will be hurt. But what is—"

"It's better not to ask what you were gonna ask. If it works, maybe I can make it work for Valencia Jones, too."

His face brightened beneath the low light of the bare bulbs. His desperation to get out of the hole he and Zak had dug for everyone was beginning to wear on him as well. The late-season blizzard had kept him out of work for an extra day, but he had called in sick the last two days. Someone needed to stir the pot and I meant for that someone to be me.

"When would you like to make these calls?" Guppy was eager to know. "I will need several minutes of preparation."

"Tonight, preferably when Zak and Johnny are asleep."

*   *   *

There was a yawn, a pause, then: "Hello."

"Tess."

"Dylan!"

"Shhhhh, keep it down."

"Are you all right? There are cops—"

"I know, Tess. I'm fine. And no, I didn't do it."

"You couldn't, Dylan, not what they say you did."

"I loved her." That was met with reverent silence. Tess was great like that. "Listen—"

"I'll go get Jeffrey."

"Don't! I called for you. Zak is alive. He's with—"

Her voice cracked. "Can I speak to him?"

She began crying. I heard her put her hand over the phone's mouthpiece, but joy was a difficult thing to cover up.

"Tess . . .Tess, you okay?"

"Never better," she sniffled.

"He can't talk to you now, but he'll be home soon."

"What about you?"

"Forget about me. Just tell everyone Zak's okay. And tell my brother I know about Hernandez."

"But—"

I hung up before she could put Jeff on the line or talk me into or out of anything. I waited for Guppy to give me the go ahead for the second call.

He tapped on the radiator and I picked up. The phone number I had given him was already ringing.

"You have reached . . ." the message began.

"Larry!" I screamed as loudly as I dared, "Larry Feld, pick up! Pick up the goddamned phone. It's me! Larry!"

"If you leave your name, number, time you called and a brief message, I . . ."

"Larry, pick up! It's me, Dylan!"

" . . .If this is a business matter, you may reach me after 10:00 A.M. at my office. The number is . . ."

"Lar—"

"Dylan, for chrissakes! I'm here. I'm here. Wait for the message to finish."

As I waited, listening to the recorded Larry, I found myself feeling sorry that I had found him at home.

"Larry?" I screamed from nerves when the message was ended. "Are you there?"

"No, schmuck, I ran down to the deli for a cup of coffee while the message was running."

"I need help, Larry."

"Help!" He was incredulous. "You were never much for understatement, Dylan. From what my sources tell me, you need a miracle, not help."

"I need you," I said.

"For what?"

"To defend me, genius."

"I don't do miracles, Dylan."

"You gonna make me beg, Larry?"

"Maybe."

"Consider yourself begged."

"Not good enough."

"What is it, Larry? You want me to swear I'm on my knees or something?"

He giggled. "I wouldn't care if you were standing on your head."

"Then what is it?" I was really starting to regret finding him at home.

"Did you like me?" he asked.

"Did I what?"

He repeated: "Did you like me?"

"Christ, Larry, I feel like I'm in *Fiddler on the Roof.* What does it matter?"

"Maybe your future depends on it or maybe you would like your brother to defend you?"

"I didn't ask my brother. I'm asking you."

"Answer my question," he persisted.

"Yes, Larry, I liked you. What, do you think I was always sticking my neck out for you because I was Abraham Lincoln? I'm no hero. I did that shit when we were kids because you were different, driven, but not like Jeffrey. With him it was like success was preordained, like he had it coming. If I had what you had, Larry, I'd be the most famous fucking writer in the world, not some *putz* peddling his screenplay ideas like a Fuller Brush man. And you could make me laugh. That's it, you could make me laugh."

"You're not a *putz*, Dylan, but I'm real tired of owing you."

"That's the joke," I told him, "you never owed me anything."

"I'll take the case," he said almost before I finished my sentence.

"Don't you wanna know if I—"

"You didn't do it, so shut up and stop wasting my time."

"Okay."

"Dylan, just one thing. Why do you need a lawyer?"

"I want to turn myself in." The words came out, but I couldn't believe I'd said them. "There's some people I need to protect."

"This have anything to do with your nephew? Don't tell me he whacked the girl."

"Don't be an idiot, Larry."

"I have to meet you and talk," he explained, "then we can arrange terms with the cops to turn yourself in. Where are you?"

"I'm in—"

MacClough stepped out of the shadows and depressed the phone button before I could finish. I could barely make his face out in the dark, but I knew it was him. I continued to hold the mute phone to my ear like a stage prop.

"No one," MacClough whispered, taking the phone from my hand, "is turning himself in. No one."

I thought about arguing with him, but his face told me not to bother. That face of his made me think twice. MacClough wasn't an unreasonable guy. You could sway him sometimes. Then there were times, times like this, that you just knew he wasn't moving. You would have better luck lifting the Statue of Liberty on your back and walking it to Prospect Park. I was just as glad to go to bed right then. I wasn't so eager to surrender that I needed to throw myself at the cops in the middle of the night.

Cancer Face

For the first time since I'd gotten to Guppy's underground palace of Red paranoia, we ate breakfast together. I whipped up some omelets and bacon and toast, keeping Guppy as far away from the kitchen as possible. We dined in the bunker. The fact was, we had spent little if any time as a group. We all seemed far too preoccupied with our own guilts and ghosts to bother with socializing. And when we did attempt to make small talk, the small talk tended to degenerate into anger, the anger into silence, the silence into separation.

The only noise at breakfast was the scraping of silverware on cheap china. No one mentioned my phone calls or my plans of surrender, though I felt sure that Zak and Guppy had some sense of what was going on. The weather had broken finally and Guppy could no longer avoid work. With the better weather came the paper. As we ate, it sat folded and untouched like a boobytrapped centerpiece at your cousin Mary's wedding. Everybody wanted to take it home, but were afraid of what might happen if they made the first grab. I thought I caught Zak's arm twitch as if he had decided to go for it only to change his mind at the last moment.

"For chrissakes!" MacClough growled, unfolding the paper to show us the front page. "Take a gander."

I looked like hell in black and white. Sometimes I think newspapers purposefully hunt down your ugliest photo before going to press. *The Riversborough Gazette* had nearly succeeded. It wasn't my investigator's license photo—Sorry, MacClough. It wasn't my bar mitzvah portrait—I'd burned all the copies. What it was was a head shot of me at Sissy Randazzo's prom. I sported an afro the size of a small asteroid, no beard, and a mustache that could have been a caterpillar, but never a moth. The grainy reproduction made it impossible to differentiate between my acne and freckles. The lapels on my polyester tux were piped in dark felt and wider than the thirteenth and fourteenth fairways at Augusta. The ruffles on my shirt added three inches to my chest and my bow tie looked like two yield signs welded together. The fact that one of my eyes was half closed when the picture was taken did nothing to enhance my already splendid visage and attire. It did, however, make me look like an escapee from an Ed Wood movie.

And all along I was thinking that Sissy Randazzo had forgiven me for grabbing her nipples that night and pretending to tune in Radio Free Europe. You never can tell. On the other hand, as Guppy was quick to point out, no one would ever recognize me now from that picture. We all actually had a pretty good laugh at my old self. MacClough stopped laughing first. We were quiet again.

"What?"

"They think you're here," Johnny said.

"Here!" Guppy was disbelieving.

Zak jumped up. "Let's get—"

"Not in this house," MacClough shoved Zak back down in his seat. "In Riversborough."

"So what?" I was curious. "We know that from TV."

"From what it says here, the cops are thinking of starting a house to house for you now that the weather's calmed down."

"I'm safe down here," I said.

MacClough sneered: "Yeah, Hitler had the same idea."

"Maybe I should not go to work."

"No!" Johnny and I chimed. "You go. We can't afford to raise any suspicions," he finished.

Then something hit me. I don't know, it was like stepping into a hole that was camouflaged by fallen leaves. You're not expecting to fall and all of a sudden boom, you're down.

"Why?" I asked.

"Why what, Uncle Dylan?"

"Why here?"

"Why here what?" Guppy joined in.

"Don't mind him," MacClough teased, "the pressure's gettin' to him."

"No. Listen, we've been going round and around, asking ourselves a thousand questions, but not getting the answers we need. Why do you think that is? It's because we haven't been asking the right question."

"So," Zak wondered, "what's the right question?"

"Why here?" I repeated.

"Jesus, that shit again."

"Why Riversborough?" I screamed at MacClough. "Why here? What makes Riversborough the Isotope capital of the northeast? What's here? Come on guys, what's here?

"The school," Zak said.

"The ski resorts," Guppy added.

"Canada," MacClough chimed in unenthusiastically.

"Exactly.," I counted off on my fingers."The school, ski resorts, and Canada's just a few miles north of here."

John was unimpressed. "So what? There must be twenty places in northern New York within pissing distance of Canada that have schools and resorts of one kind or another. Look at Plattsburgh."

"But Valencia Jones didn't go to the state university at Plattsburgh. She wasn't arrested for drug smuggling leaving a ski resort near Plattsburgh. No one in Plattsburgh felt threatened enough by our presence to have people murdered, MacClough. No one felt they had to burn down a ski resort in—"

"Okay," he relented, "you've made your point, but how does this get us any closer to anything?"

"Guppy, you think you can find out who owns Cyclone Ridge and the Old Watermill?"

"When I arrive home from work, I will set out to accomplish what you ask. I believe I should be able to get into some systems which will—"

"Yes or no?" I cut him off.

"Probably."

"I'll settle for probably."

Guppy thought about expanding on his answer, but one look at MacClough and me convinced him to skip it. He excused himself and went off to work. Johnny admonished him to keep his eyes and ears open and to try and get hold of the New York City papers. When Guppy had gone, we finished our breakfasts and passed the paper around.

"I know who owns the Old Watermill," Zak said almost sheepishly.

"You do?" I asked. "Who?"

"The school."

"The school!" MacClough puzzled. "Your school?"

"My school."

MacClough was skeptical. "I never heard of such a thing. You sure?"

I answered for Zak and explained how it made perfect sense for a college to own a hotel, particularly in a small town. Schools often have to put visiting faculty up for a few days or for a few months. On parents' weekends, you could guarantee a large number of rooms. I confessed that I had never thought Riversborough the kind of school that needed its own hotel. Usually, it was the sports powerhouse schools that invested in hotels.

"So," MacClough's voice smiled, "if colleges can own hotels, they can own ski resorts, right?"

"Holy shit!" Zak and I exclaimed in unison.

"My thoughts exactly," Johnny winked. "Holy fuckin' shit indeed." Now I almost wished the Guppster had hung around.

*　　　*　　　*

I hadn't noticed myself in the mirror since . . . in days, anyway. Maybe it was that glorious reproduction of Sissy Randazzo's prom picture that moved me to do it, to take a look. Maybe it was about time to face the truth about things, about my future or lack thereof. I'd like to think it was simply because my beard was getting scruffy and itchy and I needed a shave.

A lost face stared back at me, lonesome, childish almost. But for the beard it was my face at four. I was four when we first found out about my dad. Well, we found out he was sick. With what, we weren't told. But its name was whispered in dark corners when my parents thought they were alone. It's funny how parents try to protect themselves by protecting you. That was the face, the cancer face, the word whispered in the dark. I was lost then, too.

Most of the superficial scratches had already faded so that they were just traces now. I guess you can't force a dead hand to scratch with the same enthusiasm as a live one might in anger. The deeper cuts had begun to scab over. Very attractive and not too obvious to a blind man. I shaved my beard off. And I was fully four years old again; wide, sad eyes and chubby-cheeked. But back then, I didn't know my eyes were blue. I swear to God, I assumed they were brown. What do four-year-olds know from blue eyes? To me, the world had brown eyes like my father. It was good to have the beard off. I was tired of hiding from myself, even more so than from the authorities.

Staring into the mirror, my face morphed into Kira's. The details of her face were sketchy to me. I hadn't had the time to know it, its range of expressions, its lines and creases. What I had of it, all I would ever have of it, would have to be enough. And I vowed to the faces in the mirror, all the faces—my beardless face, cancer face, and Kira's— that I would find some reason in her death even if finding it meant sacrificing myself in the process. You know the kind of promise. You've read the words in a hundred cheesy novels. You've heard them spoken in twenty cheesy movies. But the words I spoke were not empty words. Some promises are meant to be kept.

Another Planet

The end began with Guppy's most elegant exclamation: "He's gone!"

Guppy had gotten back from work at 7:00 P.M. with a bag of groceries and the New York City papers. He seemed edgy, which was saying something for Guppy. With his dark puppy-dog eyes and calm, sweet expression, he often appeared unaffected by the pressure. Not tonight. It was as if he had sensed what was coming. His report to John and me about the Riversborough scuttlebutt was terse and discouraging.

The cops had tracked down the trucker who'd given me the lift back into town. And after coming up dry north of the border, the cops were now prepared to believe I was still in the vicinity of Riversborough. They had, as John had earlier mentioned, begun canvassing whole sections of town. It wouldn't be long, Guppy said, before they got to his neighborhood. We agreed that the cops, lacking a warrant, were unlikely to find the old bomb shelter. Even so, Guppy was unnerved.

"For chrissakes," MacClough prodded, "if there's somethin' else, you gotta tell us now. We can't afford for the cops to show up here and catch us with our pants around our ankles."

"I am afraid," he said, "that we are in danger of being found out."

"Why?" I was more than curious. "How?"

"Apparently, it has raised some suspicions with the constabulary that the waiter at the Manhattan Court Coffee House remembered me speaking with you that day and that you asked after me."

"Coincidence," MacClough dismissed. "Klein musta talked to a hundred people since he got here. I don't think the cops suspect any of them."

"Unfortunately, Mr. MacClough, I don't think you are fully aware of all the specifics. You see, Mr. Klein came to me the day of the murder. A woman customer reported seeing him at the bookstore only a short while after he left."

MacClough's face soured. "Shit!"

"By your expression," said Guppy, "I can see you understand the full implications of these two incidents."

"Is this guy from India or another planet?" MacClough wondered half-jokingly. "I was a fuckin' NYPD detective. Of course I understand. We gotta get you outta here, Klein, and fast. You," he pointed to Guppy, "get Zak and tell him he's got five minutes to get his ass in gear."

"But—" Guppy began.

"But nothin'. There's a good shot the cops are gonna show up here with a warrant in hand. I wouldn't be surprised if there's an unmarked car sitting out front right now. So move," John shouted at our host.

This time, Guppy did not question John's reasoning and ran to fetch my nephew. MacClough and I just stared at one another. What was there to say? I knew that my life as a free man was about to end.

"I'm just going to give myself up."

"Christ, Klein, not that shit again."

"No, John, I have to. I'm not going to get caught slinking around. I owe it to Kira to tell my story with my head up. If they catch me trying to escape, no one will listen. The whole world'll think I'm guilty."

"The whole world already does."

"I'm sorry, MacClough, I've gotta do this." I started to move to the bulkhead door.

He grabbed me, straining more than he should have to to hold on. I noticed his skin and the whites of his eyes were jaundiced. I wanted to ask him what was the matter, but I knew he wouldn't tell me. He had something to say and he meant for me to hear it.

"Listen, Dylan." That got my attention. He only called me that when he was serious. "I guess maybe I understand about you wanting to turn yourself in. I wanted to do it after the Hernandez case, but your brother talked me out of it. And he was right to do it. It was the right thing for me and it was the right thing for the department."

"So, you did kill him."

"That's for another telling," he said.

157

"You're not my brother, John, and I didn't kill anyone. So let go of me and let me do what I have to do."

"Can't you figure out what I'm tryin' to say? You can't give yourself up, because they'll never let you live long enough to tell your story. There won't be any arraignment or trial. They'll find you hanging in your cell before the sun comes up. Or maybe some vigilante will whack you on the way into the station. Maybe the the local cops'll shoot you and claim you went for one of their guns. It's been known to happen. Whoever's behind this has power and influence. And if they went this far to stop you, they can't afford to let you have your day in court. You walk into that police station and you're sentencing yourself to death."

"I'll do it through Larry—"

"Bad idea. Too late, anyhow."

"Maybe we're over-reacting," I proposed halfheartedly. "We don't know how long the cops questioned Guppy for. Maybe he took their questions the wrong way. If the cops really suspected him, wouldn't they have barged in here already?"

"You're whistling in the graveyard, Klein." MacClough knocked my theory down. "They wouldn't barge in. They'd have no way of knowing whether you were armed or how heavily armed. They wouldn't know if you and the Gupster were here alone or whether you had reinforcements. No, they'd wait for you and grab you on the way out."

"You mean kill me on the way out."

"Maybe, but not likely, not unless you resisted. They'd probably wait until they had you in private."

"God, that's a comfort."

MacClough pulled his .38 and signaled me to be quiet. The bulkhead door flew open and a panicked Guppy stepped through.

"He's gone!"

"Who's g—"

"Zak!" Guppy gasped. "Zak is nowhere to be found in the house."

"What is it with the fuckin' Kleins, the gene for martyr-dom dominant in your family or what?" Johnny's face twisted with worry and what looked to be hints of pain.

"Guppy, can you run through all those Isotope Web sites and chat rooms?"

"I thought we were in a rush?"

"We are," Johnny said, "but do it anyway."

I knew the way MacClough thought. He was looking for something specific. And after only two minutes of scanning, Guppy found what MacClough had been hunting for.

"Oh my god!" Guppy barely got the words out. "Look."

This is what he pointed to on the screen:

> Your nephew's here for a visit. Love Valencia. He
> says there is no disc, but we cannot take that risk.
> Bring it inn and we'll trade you for him. If not, he'll
> fade away.

Their mispelling of "inn" was not lost on us. One or all of us were about to jump into the lion's mouth to pull Zak's head out.

Training Wheels

When I came in, MacClough was standing behind Guppy, his yellowish hands enveloping the caramel skin of Guppy's hand. Guppy's hands were draped around the blueblack gun-metal of MacClough's old .38. In unison, they repeated the steps of releasing the safety, pulling back the hammer, and firing. I winced as the hammer struck. There was nothing but a click. Johnny had emptied the cylinder.

"You got it?" he asked his student.

"Yes," Guppy answered with no confidence.

As MacClough reloaded the pistol, he told Guppy to go over the plan. Dutifully, Rajiv repeated his part in our hastily designed escape.

"Everybody ready?" MacClough didn't really want an answer.

Guppy and I lied that we were.

"Okay, Klein, into the broom closet."

"Good luck, guys."

"Go to hell." MacClough winked and patted my cheek affectionately.

"I'll save you a seat."

"More likely I'll be savin' one for you."

He closed the door on me. As he did so, I caught a glimpse of Guppy's face over John's shoulder. He was scared.

Dank and claustrophobic, the broom closet felt like a coffin with training wheels. An empty bottle of Soft Scrub was my only friend. It could have been worse; the kitchen sink might've been closer to the back door. I don't even want to think about how I would have had to contort myself to get under there.

As I listened to MacClough's and Guppy's steps fade away, I visualized how the scene might play itself out. At the threshold of the front door, John stares into Guppy's eyes, promising him things will be all right. Guppy believes him. John has the gift of transferable confidence. He could almost will you to believe. I believed, somewhere. Guppy says he's ready and John pats his shoulder. MacClough reminds

Guppy of what he needs to do. Guppy, sage and brilliant, is annoyed at MacClough's constant reminders. John likes the anger in Guppy's black eyes. He likes the people he works with to have an edge to them.

MacClough takes three deep breaths; not two, not four, three. They're breaths so deep you'd swear he was going to the chair. Then, without a word, MacClough, hiding his face with a ski mask and hood, bursts out the door in to the front yard. He heads for Guppy's car. The cops, startled and caught unprepared, draw their weapons, but not before MacClough's in the driver's seat. One cop, a rookie, takes a shot. The Subaru's back windshield shatters. Angry shouts of "Cease fire!" can be heard in the next county. There's a second shot. It misses completely.

Guppy, pleading for help, stumbles out the front door, down the steps. He aims above the Subaru and squeezes off a shot. Bewildered, the cops charge across the street toward Guppy. MacClough burns rubber down the driveway and does a one-eighty in the street. The cops stop in their tracks. Some race back to their cars. Some race to Guppy. MacClough heads off into the night. The cops head off after him, squawking on their radios about Dylan Klein's mad dash in a stolen Subaru.

Guppy, gasping for air, acts dazed, shocky. He mutters something about the hospital, an ambulance and how Klein had mentioned making a run for the border. There's more squawking on the radio. An ambulance is called. Roadblocks are set up. Guppy passes out. Sirens dominate the night air. An ambulance pulls up. Guppy's loaded onto a gurney, rolled into the ambulance, and shipped off to Riversborough General. As the ambulance pulls away, one detective asks another if he should search the interior of the premises. The more senior detective gives it a moment's thought. He balks at the idea. There will be plenty of time to collect evidence after Klein is caught. He waves a uniform over and tells him to tape off the area and to stand guard when he finishes. By the time the uniform begins to cordon off the perimeter, I've already slipped out the back door.

My visualizing comes to an abrupt end when the real gunfire begins. Three shots sound like a thousand when you're alone in the dark. I don't know how to pray anymore or to whom, but I fake my way through it. There is a lull in the gunplay and I can hear Guppy's cries for help. I push open the broom closet door. Suddenly, it doesn't seem so bad in here. I get ready to run. The back door's open. The cold, fresh air is sweet in my nostrils. I run. When I stop to breathe again, Guppy's back fence is a memory. It worked. God damn it, John's plan worked. But standing there in someone's backyard, I have never felt more naked in my life.

*   *   *

I could barely hear the sirens anymore by the time I got to the Old Watermill Inn. There was no police activity here that I could see. From a convenient shadow I watched people drift in and out of the hotel. Business as usual at the Old Watermill, murder or no murder. Even in little towns, memories are short. Life goes on. It felt unholy to me that it should. Maybe, I thought, that was what was wrong with the world. Trauma ran off our collective shoulders like so much rainwater. In an insane world, our drive for a sense of normalcy was inversely proportional to the tragedy heaped upon us. But I could have been wrong. Things might only have appeared normal from the distance the shadows afforded me. Knowing Riversborough, there might well have been a shiny new plaque affixed to the old inn during my brief absence: "The best little crime scene this side of the border."

Stepping around to the side entrance, I noticed several posters of my kisser tacked up on a utility pole like fliers for a weekend yard sale. Unfortunately, these were not reproductions of Sissy Randazzo's revenge. This picture actually looked like me. I waited a bit before going in, but not too long. The time MacClough's mad dash would buy me was not unlimited. He didn't figure to outrun the cops in Guppy's ancient Subaru forever. Now it was my turn to take the three deep breaths.

The hallway ice machine didn't seem at all surprised by my presence. I could only hope its blasé attitude about my being there would carry over to the warm-blooded members

162

of the hotel's staff. The first test of my anonymity was coming up the hall in the shape of a young couple. He was jingling the room keys in his hand. She was jingling something else. I cleared my throat to save them a bit of embarrassment. It also caused them to look away as they approached. They wished me good evening as they passed and giggled all the way to their room.

I took the long way round to the ever-vacant guest lounge. It was dimly lit as usual and it gave me a good view of the front desk. He was there, the scum who had helped to murder Kira. Life went on for him, too, but not for very much longer. I hadn't discussed my plans for him with Guppy or MacClough. I knew they would try to talk me out of it, but I meant to kill that cocksucker before the sun rose in the sky. And I meant to make it painful and bloody. I could barely stop myself from breaking a piece of glass and charging him. I would cut his throat with the jagged wedge of glass. Then, as he fought in vain to plug the red river flowing out of his jugular, I'd snap the glass in half and shove the pieces into his mouth. As I pounded his cheeks against the thick walnut front desk, the glass would shatter. He'd swallow some of it, washed down with a chaser of his own blood. The big shards would shred his face from the inside out. And just before he lost consciousness, I would . . .

"Excuse me," a gentle, foreign voice called to me from a corner of the dark room, "but can you give me the correct time."

Turning to a leather wing chair, I could make out the figure of the man who needed the time, but not much else about him. He was short, svelte, and dressed in a suit. He seemed lost in the big chair. I apologized for not being able to help him. I did not say that I had murder on my mind.

"I am sorry to have bothered you," he bowed slightly.

"No bother," I lied, but I was intrigued by his voice. He was Asian, but clearly comfortable with American English.

"I have made the trip across the Pacific many times, but have never learned to reset my watch."

"You'll get it eventually," I assured him, trying to turn back to the front desk.

"No. I fear I shall never make this trip again. I have loved your country, but I can never return to it."

I could not help but be drawn to him. "Why not, the INS giving you a rough time?

He laughed sadly. "Nothing like that, no. Do you know what I like most about Americans? They can enjoy themselves without self-consciousness, without artifice, without approval of the group. You enjoy to drink, but don't need to drink. You go to a club and enjoy karaoke, but would be fine without it. You can be individuals. In Japan, we have achieved many great things against great odds, but we are not comfortable with ourselves as individuals. Do you know what we do to those who wear their individualism on their sleeves?"

"You beat them down like a nail that sticks out of a board." I recalled what Kira had said.

"Exactly so," he bowed again. "You know Japan?"

"No," I said, "I had a teacher who knew both countries and was wise in spirit."

He said nothing immediately. There was a stifled gasp somewhere in the darkness. There is nothing particularly sad about hearing a man cry. But to hear him struggle to hold tears back, that is the essence of sadness.

"Are you okay?" I tried to distract him.

"Yes, yes. It is just that my daughter was such a woman as your teacher; torn between two countries and wise in spirit. Now I come to take her home to Japan, but it was never a home to her. I don't know whether she can ever truly rest there."

I needed the wall to hold me upright. And just as in my dream, the world fell out from beneath my feet. The world was doing that a lot, lately. This was Kira's father. It was as if we were standing at opposite ends of a black void, connected but apart. If a pin were to prick the vacuum, we would be drawn together, colliding at the speed of light.

"She will rest," I assured him. "She will rest."

"Thank you. Maybe we can speak again."

"I would like that," I said. "We have things to share."

He stood. Bowed at where I was standing and moved quietly out of the room.

When I turned back to the front desk, the clerk was gone. A new face was on duty. So much for shards of glass. The world back under my feet, I walked out of the lounge the way I'd come in. Just through the doorjamb, a shape stepped out in front of me. By the time I recognized it, a gun barrel was buried in my ribs.

"Come on, Mr. Klein, we don't want to be late for your appointment."

Piece of Skirt

We walked for a little bit—me, the desk clerk, and the ski dude—down into the basement of the Old Watermill. It was musty as hell and made me pine for Guppy's broom closet. The three of us had little to say. There was no need. The ski dude's gun barrel communicated to me speed and direction. I did ask if it was possible for the ski dude not to press his pistol completely through my ribs. He responded by pressing harder. I would remember never to beg him for mercy.

We stopped by a door marked "Storage Room" and I wondered aloud if this was where the desk clerk changed into Superman. That earned me a smack in the back of my head with the gun butt. That was one way to get the damn thing out of my ribs. When I reached up to feel the lump on my head, they pushed me through the door. I landed chin first. That pissed me off and I spat in the desk clerk's face when he bent over me. Now the square face of the 9 mm Glock was pressed against my teeth. Suddenly, I thought, my ribs weren't such a bad place for the barrel of a gun after all.

The ski dude just stood above me smiling down. He enjoyed his work just a bit too much for my comfort. In the meantime, the desk clerk frisked me, patting down every spot on my body, turning all my pockets out.

"He doesn't have it on him," he said to the ski dude.

"Of course I don't have the disc on me, you fucking moron." I got the words out pretty well considering there was a gun in my mouth. "When I get my nephew, you'll get your disc."

Ski dude pulled the gun away and yanked me up like I was filled with helium. I didn't miss the gun. And it was nice to breathe again. The desk clerk gave a nod to his accomplice. Ski dude smiled. I knew I wasn't going to enjoy this. A fist buried itself in my gut so hard that my liver French-kissed my right kidney. Some foul-tasting liquid flew out of my mouth. I didn't know what it was, but I knew it was the type of fluid that was supposed to stay inside the human body. I didn't have a chance to dwell on my body fluids very long. Unconsciousness has a way of distracting me.

To wake up running through an inventory of the parts of your body that ache is usually a bad omen of things to come. My mouth still tasted of the mystery fluid and the slice on my chin was still bleeding, so I guessed I hadn't been out that long. My liver was back in place, but I felt bruised from the inside out.

I was lying face-down on a concrete slab and when I tried to push myself up, the back of my head nearly exploded. It didn't do wonders for the contents of my stomach, either. I opted for rolling over onto my back. I managed that without too much discomfort. There was a string of bare bulbs dangling above my head. They swayed as if blown by a breeze I could not feel. There were space heaters placed along the base of the unpainted concrete walls. The walls themselves were not flat, but concave. The place had the feel of a construction sight.

After several minutes on my back, I inched over to a wall and used its gentle slope to ease myself into a sitting position. My head voted against the upright posture, but came around to my way of thinking after punishing me with thirty seconds of extreme nausea and pain. When the wave passed, I felt I recognized my prison. The tunnels beneath the college were of the same dimensions. I was unnerved by the deathly silence of the place. Having grown up in a bedroom above a boiler, around the corner from one of Brooklyn's busiest thoroughfares and one block away from Coney Island Hospital's emergency room, I had always been uncomfortable with silence. Okay, when I was writing, I wanted silence. When I was bleeding, I wanted some noise.

I stood up and walked the tunnel, up and back. I was in a section about sixty paces long closed at both ends by plywood walls. One wall had a locked, spring-loaded door in it. I did some requisite banging and screaming after which I did some requisite puking. At least now there was some stink to go along with the silence. I got horizontal once again and willed myself to pass out, but even that yielded mixed results. I dreamed I was in pain.

Someone was slapping my cheeks the next time I opened my eyes. Just what a man with a cracked head and a sliced-up face needs. I thrust my left arm out at where I thought the slapper's throat might be and latched onto the first bit of flesh I could find. Hearing choking and feeling hands grab my left wrist, I congratulated myself for good aim.

"Uncle Dylan! Uncle Dylan!" were words I thought I heard through the choking and gasps for air.

I let go, but, in all honesty, not without some regret. Deep in the pit of my stomach, I continued to be furious with Zak for his manipulations. I was never very good at math, but no matter how I turned the equation around, Zak's pulling at the puppet strings still resulted in Kira's murder. I suppose that as a younger, more narcissistic man, I might have seen things differently. I might have thought my few days with Kira were somehow worth it. I wasn't that good a liar anymore. My joy, no matter how expansive, would never be worth someone else's life.

"Are we in the tunnels beneath the school?" I asked, sitting up.

"Yeah," Zak said, rubbing his throat. "But these tunnels are unused. They are extensions to buildings that were never built. Everybody knows they exist, but none of the students know how to get access."

"Now you do, but I don't think it's worth it."

"I guess not," he agreed.

"How did—" My question was cut short by an opening door.

"I put him here, Mr. Klein," a vaguely familiar voice answered my unfinished question. Dean Dallenbach stepped through the open door. He was flanked on either side by the desk clerk and the ski dude. "Now why don't you make the inevitable easy on everyone and hand over the disc."

"If it existed, asshole," I didn't hesitate, "I might be inclined to make it easy."

"You *are* going to be tiresome, aren't you?" Dallenbach's hand gestures were very affected, exaggerated.

"I guess so."

"But we've already been through this with your nephew, Mr. Klein. Do you actually believe me such a fool?"

I smiled. "You really want an answer to that?"

"George!" Dallenbach barked.

The ski dude hopped to and proceeded to slap me so hard across the face that the force tore a gash in my cheek.

"Nice shot, George, but you're pissing me off. I get very stubborn when I get pissed off."

"Jerry!" the Dean was barking again. "Hold Mr. Klein steady for George this time. I don't think our guest quite appreciates the seriousness of the position he and his nephew are in."

As the desk clerk stepped toward me, I thought I saw him lick his lips. But he was a phony motherfucker. With him it was all show for the boss' sake. And I knew Jerry would be a little more careless than his partner. While he moved by me to take hold of me, I head-butted Jerry in a part of his anatomy that was particularly sensitive to strong blows with a blunt object. He folded like a pup tent in a tornado. And as he was busily getting in touch with his new vocal range, I sprang on top of him, sinking my teeth into his neck. But just as I was clamping through the thick sheath around his jugular, I heard Zak scream.

"Your nephew's about to lose his resemblance to you, Mr. Klein," Dean Dallenbach warned almost too calmly. "I suggest you get off of Jerry this instant."

I rolled off and got a kick in the ribs for my trouble. It was worth it. Jerry looked like Christmas; red and green all at once. He had one hand on his balls and one on his neck. George smiled at me. That took all the fun out of things. I knew no good would come of his smile. He teased me by releasing his arm from around Zak's neck. But just as Zak was out of his grip, George pistol-whipped Zak across the back of his head. It was one of George's specialties. I knew from first hand experience.

Zak went down harder than Jerry, blood spurting through his thick, reddish brown hair.

"Have I established my intentions, Mr. Klein? I'm quite certain you can be very stubborn and very brave when it comes to pain. But I know the type of students that attend this school and somehow I don't get the impression that your nephew, as motivated as he might be, could withstand what you could, sir." His assessment was twin to mine. "And even if he were able to muster what it would take to put up with

George's skills, I doubt that you would be able to sit through it. Now please hand over the disc."

I never got a chance to debate the issue. The door swung open behind Dallenbach and MacClough, hands cuffed behind him and blood leaking from the corners of his mouth, was shoved through. Except for the blood, MacClough seemed well enough. I thought I detected a smile. He had apparently enjoyed his little escapade. He didn't let anyone else catch wind of his pleasure and got properly serious when he saw Zak face down on the concrete.

Two of Riversborough's finest stepped in quickly behind John and closed the door. One of the cops looked like an escapee from a blimp factory and had a nose so full of gin blossoms he could have opened a florist shop. He wore a tired yellow toupee, had yellow fingers with dirty nails and incongruously square white teeth. I doubted the teeth were original equipment. His partner was a fidgety boy with slicked-back hair and eyes that couldn't agree on which way to look. In most places he would have been lucky to get a job as a security guard. In Riversborough, he'd probably make commissioner.

"I don't like it," said the future commissioner to no one in particular. "I don't like it."

"You're not getting paid for your opinion," Dallenbach hissed. "Now get out of here and go tell your story about Mr. MacClough's escape to any fool who will listen."

The fat cop was busily cleaning a few pounds of dirt from under his nails with a key. He wasn't the excitable type. His manicure complete, he tossed the key to Dallenbach. "For the cuffs," he said.

Dallenbach immediately tossed the keys to George. Jerry frowned, truly hurt that his boss had chosen George to hold the keys. The cops left. As the door closed behind them, we could hear the fidgety boy still moaning about his work.

"These two I recognize," MacClough nodded at George and Jerry. "That's the asshole who followed you from the airport and that's the desk clerk from the Old Watermill. But who's—"

"John MacClough, meet Dean Dallenbach," I introduced them.

"I know all about Mr. MacClough," Dallenbach doffed an imaginary hat. "Join us, won't you?"

"For a man who's about to take a tumble, you're in an awfully jolly fuckin' mood," MacClough sneered.

The smile ran away from Dallenbach's face. Zak stirred, sitting up. He rubbed the back of his head. I pulled him to his feet. If the three of us were going to try anything, Zak would be better off in an upright position.

"George!" Dallenbach made a gun out of his thumb and index finger and pointed at Zak. George pressed his Glock to Zak's temple. "The disc. We were talking about the disc."

"There is no—" Zak began.

"Stop it, Zak," MacClough cut him off. "There's no use in jerking these guys around anymore. They're way too smart to believe that they got played for fools by some college kid."

"You're annoying me, Mr. MacClough."

"Good, I'm tryin' to."

George broke into a smile, but Dallenbach told him to calm down. John had bought us a little time.

"Where is the disc?" Dallenbach repeated, but, for the first time, there was a trace of doubt in his voice.

"Not so fast," MacClough played his hand. "After you satisfy my curiosity, maybe we'll talk about the disc. And do me a favor, don't even say that I'm in no position to bargain. If I wasn't, we'd all be dead by now."

Dallenbach did the finger gun thing again and had George move the real gun to John's temple.

"Kill me, asshole, go ahead. You see, the problem is, I'm the only one who knows where the disc is. I had it with me when I ran and ditched it on the way out of town."

"You're bluffing." Dallenbach squirmed.

"Then call the bluff. You're gonna whack us anyways."

I'd been in several rough situations with MacClough in the past, but he was really pushing it this time. I couldn't believe what was coming out of his mouth. It was all I could do not to tell him to try and play it a bit less over the top.

"Very well." Dallenbach gestured for Georgie boy to lower his 9mm. "What is it you want to know?"

"How'd a clown like you get involved with Isotope in the first place?" John asked.

"Your manner is starting to annoy me, Mr. MacClough."

"Slap me on the knuckles with a ruler like the sisters at St. Mark's. It didn't improve my manner any, but it made them feel better. So how'd ya get involved?"

"Weakness," Dallenbach replied matter-of-factly. "Weakness."

"That covers a lot of territory," I noted, pointing my head at George. I thought Dallenbach almost blushed. "Well, yes, I am rather fond of George's *type*." George wasn't so fond of the word 'type.' "But it was my gambling, I fear, that did me in. It is one thing to be a compulsive gambler with few resources. It is quite another to be one and have access to a well-funded school's endowment."

"But you're just a dean!" I exclaimed. "You shouldn't have—"

"But I had access to someone who had access. Money, money, money. . . ."

"But the well went dry," MacClough said.

"It always does, Mr. MacClough. My friend got faint of heart and was afraid of being found out. You see, he was using the school's purchase of the Old Watermill to cover our tracks and I got just the slightest bit greedy and asked that he divert some additional funds to cover another investment. I thought that other investment would see us through our old age and cover my debts."

"Cyclone Ridge," I said.

"Very good, Mr. Klein. Cyclone Ridge."

"That well went dry, too, and quicker than you thought," MacClough put his two cents in.

"Much too quickly. Cyclone Ridge was a dog, an albatross."

"Don't tell me," MacClough smirked, "you found some new partners."

"To be perfectly accurate, Mr. MacClough, they found me. Gamblers do tend to wear their debts on their sleeves. My creditors saw an opportunity and called in their markers. It was a set up that suited their purposes quite well. Cyclone Ridge was a perfect storehouse and transshipment point for the distribution of Isotope across Canada and the Northeast. Who would think to look for drugs in sleepy, little Riversborough? Until that fool Markham loaded the goods into the wrong BMW, the arrangement worked out rather nicely for all parties involved."

"Yeah, everyone but your old boyfriend who got you access to the endowment," John said. "It's a good bet your new partners had you dissolve your old partnership."

Dallenbach soured. "I'm afraid they insisted on it."

"What happened," I wondered, "a convenient midnight skiing accident?"

"I don't know, frankly. I didn't want to know."

I was curious. "But you did have Steven Markum killed?"

George got all happy at my question. That alone was answer enough.

"Yes," Dallenbach confirmed, "and he bloody well deserved it. If it were not for his abject stupidity, we wouldn't all be standing here. Valencia Jones would be just another student struggling with her second tier course in metaphysics."

"And Kira would still be alive," I growled.

"That's on your head, Mr. Klein. If you had spent more time looking for your nephew and less time chasing a piece of skirt, your friend would still be drawing breath. It was you who presented us with the opportunity. We simply took it."

No matter the situation, chatting reduces the level of tension in a room. That's how I managed to get my fist into Dallenbach's teeth without interference. Some of his teeth splintered. Normally, I might have felt some of the jagged enamel dig into the skin of my knuckles, but I was way too preoccupied with the bullet ripping through the top of my left shoulder to notice pieces of broken teeth. Christ, it burned like acid on fire inside me. The floor reached up and yanked me down hard. I forgot how to breathe and why. The shot's report rang in my ears.

"Not in here!" Dallenbach screamed, spitting out blood and bits of his teeth. "You nearly shot me, you fool!"

George enjoyed being called a fool almost as much as he liked being called a type.

"I just clipped him," George did speak. "And I didn't come close to hitting you."

Zak and MacClough, his hands still cuffed, came to attend to me.

"Leave him!" Dallenbach had completely lost his sense of humor. "We've wasted enough time, Mr. MacClough. Where's the disc?"

"Fuck you, asshole! There is no disc."

I winced for MacClough, expecting George to punish him for his delightful use of the English language. But George wasn't smiling, flashing his fists, nor pistol-whipping anyone just now.

"Oh, God, not that again. I warn you, my patience is at low ebb."

"It wouldn't matter if your patience were at neap tide," MacClough laughed, "there is no disc."

"If you're stalling for time, Mr. MacClough," Dallenbach said, grabbing the 9mm out of George's hand, "you needn't bother. The cavalry isn't coming. I'm afraid that DEA agent who's been following Mr. Klein about had a rather nasty accident in the fire at Cyclone Ridge. Unless you've got an in with Ezekiel, and can conjure up charred bones, no one's coming to your rescue." Dallenbach ejected a bullet from the gun's chamber for dramatic purposes, pointed it at Johnny's heart and began counting backwards from ten: "Ten . . . nine . . .eight . . . seven . . .six . . . five . . . four . . . three . . . two—"

The spring-loaded door flew open, clanging against the wall. Zak and John jumped. I was already so wired that I barely reacted. Dallenbach, however, and his two boys seemed unfazed. I thought I saw Dallenbach check his watch. Two men—one dressed in a loose-fitting trench coat, the other in a full-length vicuna coat—came into the tunnel.

"You're late," Dallenbach tapped his wrist.

"Fuck you!" vicuna coat said, "these fuckin' tunnels get me all whacky. It's like a fuckin' sci-fi movie down here, people livin' in tunnels and shit. Hey," he screwed up his face, "what the fuck happened to your face, you suckin' on concrete lollipops or what?"

"One of your partners?" John surmised.

"Actually, Mr. Lippo's one of their representatives. How

ever did you guess?" Dallenbach wondered, tongue in cheek.

"With that vocabulary it had to be a toss-up between a wise-guy and Werner Von Braun. Since Von Braun's dead . . ."

"Shut the fuck up!" Lippo ordered. "These the guys?"

"Those three, yes," Dallenbach confirmed, "but not yet. They have some information I need."

"Bullshit! The boss says I gotta whack 'em, I whack 'em. He didn't say nothin' about waitin' time. And you," he glared at Dallenbach, "I'm supposed to teach you a lesson."

"What," the dean's voice was breaking, "could you possibly teach me?"

Lippo looked at Zak, Johnny, and me. "Which one of youz girlfriend's got whacked?"

"Me," I said, propping myself up.

"That shouldn't'a happened," Lippo said. "That was sloppy like every other fuckin' thing around here."

"Thanks for the sympathy."

"Gino!" Lippo snapped his fingers and held out his hand. Gino placed a .38 police special in Lippo's hand. "Here!" Lippo held the gun out to me. "Go ahead, kill either one a those two pricks. And don't get no ideas. Gino boy'll cut you down before you fart the wrong way."

Suddenly, my left shoulder didn't hurt so much. I took the gun and swung the tip of the barrel between George and Jerry. George looked particularly unhappy, but not especially frightened. Jerry, on the other hand, was a whisper away from begging. I picked Jerry. Dying at my hand would have no special significance to George.

"Okay," Dallenbach threw his hands up, "I get the point. We shall endeavor to be more careful in the future. Now take that gun away from Klein and let's get on with this."

"You don't get it, do you?" Lippo puzzled. "I ain't jokin'. Go ahead and kill the prick," he urged me.

Dallenbach was sweating now.

"Don't!" MacClough shouted. "Don't do it, Klein. It'll stay with you forever."

I pulled the hammer back on the .38.

"They're gonna kill us, Dylan. You're just makin' it easier for them to have it look like we all went down in a gunfight between us and Dallenbach's boys."

"Hey, shut the fuck up," Lippo warned MacClough.

"Don't, Dylan!"

I began to nudge the trigger toward me. Bang! The shot went off and I went down, MacClough on top of me. The slug ricocheted off the concrete. Everyone hit the floor who wasn't there already. A light bulb exploded, its glass sprinkling down. The .38 was out of my hand. It was a long few seconds.

"Get up!" Lippo demanded.

We obliged. But when we got up, the .38 was in Jerry's shaking right hand. He pointed it at the spot where Lippo's vicuna coat fell away from his heart. Lippo ignored him, brushing the concrete dust off his lavish overcoat.

"Goddammit! I just had this thing cleaned."

And as he finished his sentence, there was a sort of muffled spitting sound, a puff of smoke, and Jerry collapsed backwards. He lay all twisted like an ill-constructed jigsaw puzzle, a look of utter surprise on his dead face. Blood pooled where his right eye used to be.

"The other one, too," Lippo said almost too nonchalantly.

George smiled, began laughing in an odd, strangled sort of way. He was not going to go quietly into that good night. He charged. He didn't get too far; three feet maybe. But because he had been a moving target, Gino hadn't managed to make clean work of it. The belly of George's skin-tight ski suit was a crimson mess. He writhed in pain on the floor, trying to hold his guts in place. Lippo calmly removed his coat, handing it to Gino, and grabbed the Glock out of Dallenbach's fear-frozen right hand. He placed his shoe on George's throat and pressed down hard enough to steady George's twisting.

"Here's dessert," Lippo said, placing the gun barrel to George's heart. "Prick!"

As the shot went off a wave went through George's body. I almost expected the floor to shake. Dallenbach was white. I'm not sure whether it was fear or grieving or what.

"I really do get the lesson now," he managed to say. "So, can we please get on with it?"

"I'm a cop," MacClough said. "You wanna kill a cop?"

"Retired over ten years ago," Dallenbach, feeling more his old self, retorted. "No one will send out the National Guard, if your body should turn up."

"I don't like whackin' cops. My brother-in-law's on the job. But this ain't my headache. C'mon," he said, waving the 9mm at us, "let's everybody go for a nice walk."

"What about them?" Dallenbach wondered about the late George and Jerry.

"Them? Fuck them! We'll worry about them later."

"Let's listen to the man," I urged, getting to my feet. The pain in my left shoulder nearly knocking me back down. "The sooner they kill us, the sooner that disc gets to the cops."

"Disc?" Lippo stopped dead in his tracks and stared coldly at the dean. "What disc?"

"You mean your partner didn't tell you about the disc that my nephew downloaded after he hacked his way into Dean Dallenbach's computer? Makes you wonder what else he didn't tell you about, doesn't it?"

"Shut up and get going," Dallenbach slapped my wounded shoulder.

"No!" Lippo disagreed. "You," he pointed to me, "talk."

"Don't you know what all this is about? My nephew used to date that girl that's on trial for muling the Isotope. The details of how he hacked the system are irrelevant, but let's just say that there's a disc somewhere out there that details your distribution system and implicates your bosses. Now, my nephew's no idiot. He knew what his life would be worth if he took the disc directly to the cops, so he's been trying to barter it for the girl's freedom for months. That's all he wanted, the girl's freedom."

"I never heard nothin' about no disc, Dallenbach."

"That's because there is no disc," he pleaded. "I didn't want to risk getting other people involved until I was sure it either did or didn't exist."

"Other people are involved, *stroonze*. You think I'm here for the climate?"

"What bullshit story did he tell your boss to get you down here, anyways?" MacClough egged Lippo on.

"I don't know, but nobody mentioned no disc."

177

"Did anybody mention the dead DEA agent?" MacClough wondered, innocent as a lamb.

"Fuck no!"

"Well, Dallenbach," I prodded, "here's your chance. I understand the mob just loves being involved with the murder of federal agents."

Working on the axiom that less is sometimes more, Dallenbach said nothing in his own defense. "Come on, Lippo, can we get this over with? We can deal with these peripheral issues later."

"Sure, Dean, we can do that for you. Hey Gino, gimme back my coat." Lippo took great care with his precious coat. "You know what happens sometimes when like McDonalds or somebody gives out a franchise to a guy who like cooks the books or don't follow company rules and shit like that?"

"I'm not sure I get your point, Lippo," Dallenbach said impatiently.

"Humor me, okay? So do you know what happens or what?"

"I imagine," Dallenbach answered, "that they reclaim their franchise."

"Right! Exactly fuckin' right. They take back their franchise. And right now, that's what we're gonna do, Dallenbach. Take back our franchise, you total fuck-up."

"I don't un—" Dallenbach began.

"You understand, asshole. You understand."

We all stepped away from Dallenbach.

"Why don't I do all of them right here?" Gino spoke up for the first time. I liked it better when he didn't talk.

"Nah," Lippo said, pointing at Dallenbach, "just him."

"But what about the disc?" Dallenbach cried in desperation.

"What about it?" Lippo was cool. "If there really is no disc, then we got nothin' to worry about. If there is a disc, who gives a fuck? I betcha me and Gino's names ain't on it. Am I right or what, Gino?"

Gino laughed at that.

Dallenbach blurted out: "But Malzone and DiMinici, your bosses will go down."

"Yeah, and so what? They ain't gonna blame me for it.

You was the one who never told them about it. And after tonight, there ain't gonna be anybody to say I knew about it. Besides, me and Gino are overdue for a promotion." Lippo nodded to Gino.

Gino's hand came up holding an Uzi with a thick silencer extended from the barrel.

"But—" Dallenbach threw his hands up.

"Look at it this way," Lippo consoled him, "we're doin' you a favor. If Malzone and DiMinici had ever found out about the disc, they wouldn't make this so quick and painless. This way you go out beggin' to live. With them, you'd go out beggin' to die. So cross yourself and shut your eyes."

Dallenbach actually took his advice.

Before Gino could do Dallenbach his favor, MacClough went down in a heap. He was in terrible pain. He was doubled over on the floor, his left leg twitching. His bottom lip was bleeding from where he was biting through it. This wasn't a feint to buy time and Lippo knew it. I tried holding John, but the pain would not let me comfort him.

Gino and Lippo studied MacClough and searched each other's eyes.

"Okay," Lippo said, "do 'em all here. We'll play some games with the guns or we'll just throw a match on the pile. The cops in this town'll be sorting it out till next Halloween."

MacClough winked at me. Gino had let him get too close. He kicked the gunman's legs out from under him and the back of Gino's head cracked hard on the concrete floor. I hit Lippo with a cross body block. My shoulder burned down through my toes, but, I thought, getting blood on Lippo's coat was almost worth it. It's funny what you think about. I stopped thinking about it when Lippo pounded the 9 mm butt into the square of my back. That wasn't a good sign. But suddenly, another body piled on. It was Zak. I couldn't see what was going on exactly, but I could feel Zak struggling with Lippo's gun hand. I wondered if MacClough and Dallenbach were sharing a cup of tea while we were scrumming about on the ground.

There was a shot. That got everyone's attention. I didn't figure it was John holding the gun. He was good, but his hands had been cuffed for quite some time and I doubted they had enough feeling left in them to handle a blind grab and behind-the-back shooting.

"Get away from him," Dallenbach ordered.

Zak and I knew who he meant. We moved away. Lippo looked almost ridiculous seated there on his ass in his dirty coat. The fact that he was still holding the Glock made him seem a bit less silly. It was Mexican stand off time between Dallenbach and Lippo. Lippo didn't wait to discuss it and squeezed off a few shots. Dallenbach crumbled. The door flew open and an endless stream of state policemen flew in behind Detective Fazio. Lippo wasn't an eloquent speaker, but he could compute the odds. He immediately tossed the Glock at Dallenbach's body and started screaming something about self-defense. Gino moaned, opened his eyes, and went back to concussionville.

Fazio, his crooked nose shiny with sweat, just stood there shaking his head at us. He was out of breath and thought smoking a Kent was the best way to catch it. He looked at MacClough's cuffed hands and John caught his gaze.

"That one's got the key," MacClough nodded at Dallenbach.

Fazio dutifully went about collecting the keys and undoing the cuffs. MacClough spent the next five minutes rubbing his wrists. Gloved hands were pushing and prodding my shoulder and the back of Zak's head. The general consensus was that we'd live.

"Did you get all that?" MacClough asked, pulling a small microphone off his inner thigh.

"Every word," Fazio said. "Every fucking word." He turned to me. "Sorry about the girl."

I had nothing in me to say to him just then, but he smiled at what he must have seen in my eyes.

"What the fuck took you so long?" MacClough griped.

"These tunnels, I'm not an ant for chrissakes! I can get you from the IND to the BMT to the IRT, but anywheres north of Syracuse I'm no good underground."

"How the—" I started the question.

"We'll talk about it some other time," Fazio winked.

A vaguely military looking gentleman in aviator sunglasses, a blond brush cut, and cheek bones higher than K2 introduced himself to me as DEA Field Supervisor Robert Rees. I shook his hand.

"Good work," he said. "Good work."

Whatever that meant. Too many people on both sides of the issue had died to make something good of it. I asked him if I might be allowed to leave now. He muttered something about my shoulder and a hospital. I told him the hospital could wait. He told one of the state troopers to take me wherever I wanted to go. He shook my hand again. Maybe he was as much in shock as the rest of us.

I asked MacClough how he was feeling. He sort of laughed at me and said that he'd live. I guessed he would. Life is a hard thing to take away from some people.

Zak put his hand out for me to pull him up. I pulled him up. There were tears in his eyes and when he began to beg forgiveness, I said he had nothing to beg for. Forgiveness wasn't my province. He had to forgive himself. My anger had all vanished in a pool of other peoples' blood. I kissed him, told him I loved him, and ordered him to go visit his grandfather's grave.

"No one'll ever call me the family fuck-up again," he vowed.

"Yeah, Zak, I know. And they don't play stickball in Milwaukee."

It fit somehow.

When I was almost through the door, MacClough called out for me: "Where you goin'?"

"There's a man at the Old Watermill Inn who I need to talk to." I didn't look back.

Poltergeists

Once again, the swimming pools and split ranches were rushing by beneath the belly of my plane.

Although it was only several weeks ago that I had flown home for my father's funeral, Hollywood felt like ancient history to me now. That's the trick of time, isn't it? It's not how much passes by, but how much happens as it passes.

As the flight attendant floated on by my row, I thought of Kira. She resembled her in only the most superficial ways—the almond eyes, the luminescent black hair. She smiled at me, checked the back of my seat to make certain of its upright position, and continued down the cabin. It was little moments like these that hurt the most, the unexpected flashes of her and the thoughts of what could have been. Sometimes it is a curse to have an active imagination.

It was also moments like these that made me wish I could believe in the God of my parents. I thought it must be a great comfort to have the faith that everything happened for some greater reason, that deaths, no matter how cruel or untimely, had a purpose we just could not understand.

I neither believed nor understood. I was alone.

Japan had been good for me. Kira's parents treated me like family and introduced me to everyone as Kira's fiancé. There was no anger in any of the family, no ugliness about the violence in America. No one felt inclined to blame me. It seemed everyone had the ability to make sense of things but me. Kira's mother, fierce and stoic, took me for a walk one day to a Shinto shrine. As we sat in a rock garden under the cold sunlight, she spoke to me about her only child. She never once looked at me, talking instead to the few birds that landed on the rocks to sun their plumes.

"My girl was never happy," she said. "To my shame, she had no footing. At first, we tried to make her too traditional. It is not an unnatural reaction, I think, to being in a foreign land. Our feet, my husband's and my own, were on wet rocks themselves. America can be overwhelming to people who are raised on sacrifice."

"You have nothing to explain to me. I should be the one," I confessed, "to explain."

"Thank you for your graciousness. These are hard things to say, but a mother has the right to say them. She was an unhappy girl; no friends, no family, moving all the time. My husband's career was consuming. So, when Kira decided to stay behind, I was . . ." She began to cry. "I was almost—"

"—relieved," I finished for her.

"Her unhappiness and our guilt was easier to deal with a continent away. In my awkward grief, what I am trying to say is that you must be a special man to have made Kira want to love you. It seemed she never wanted to love her parents."

"Mine was the easier role. You had already made her perfect."

With that, I stood and walked back to the house alone. I left Kira's mother by herself to sort things out amongst the rocks and birds. At one point, I turned back to look at her. She was my age, maybe a year or two older, but was, I thought, wiser than I would ever be and far more courageous.

At the airport, Kira's father gave me a family photo album, a handshake, and a bow. We knew we would never see one another again.

*   *   *

As always, MacClough was waiting for me outside customs. He was still heavy, but frail-looking somehow. His skin was jaundiced as it had been in Riversborough. He was worn out and looked like shit. I probably looked worse, having spent the better part of a day in the air. Although considerable creature comforts were available on board, no one would ever mistake twenty hours in a 747 for a weekend at a Palms Springs spa.

We embraced. His handshake was firm as ever. There was relief in that. We exchanged some small talk on the way through the parking lot. I continued walking even after MacClough had stopped.

"This is it," John said, pointing to a rented car.

"Where's the T-Bird?"

"I decided to finally get it fully restored. It's at a place out in Montauk that specializes in '60s Fords. It'll be done in a coupl'a weeks. Already paid for."

I thought that was an odd thing for him to tell me, but I just loaded my bags and myself inside. Near the airport, it was difficult to judge the season. It always seemed cold at the airport and the air always smelled of hot metal and spent kerosene. But with my window down slightly as we hit the Cross Island, I could smell spring coming. I could read it in the orange face of the setting sun. My eyes set more quickly than the sun.

We were off the LIE and the sky was dark when I woke up. I peeked over at MacClough, but he caught me.

"Up for the home stretch, huh?" He rubbed the back of my neck.

"I guess." I was so articulate when I awoke from sleep.

"Listen, I'm goin' away for a little while. Will you keep an eye on the Scupper for me?"

"Where you—"

"I don't know where I'm goin'," he said, "but I'm burnt. It's time to take a rest away from here."

"How long?"

"For chrissakes, Klein! Will you watch the Scupper for me or what?"

"You know I will," I threw my hands up in surrender. "What the fuck else do I have to do? Besides, it's a better gig than my agent could get me."

MacClough thought that was very funny. He didn't restart the conversation until we were nearly at the Sound Hill village limits.

"I didn't kill him, Dylan," was how he began.

"Hernandez?"

"Yeah, Hernandez. You were right about the rolled-up newspaper. I did rough him up pretty good, but he just wouldn't tell me where the Boatswain kid was."

"So you used your second gun, pulled out all but one cartridge, and stuck it in his mouth."

"Just like I learned in school," he admitted. "Even

though he thought it was a random spin of the cylinder, I knew the bullet was in the last chamber. That gave me five shots to play with."

"He talked."

"But he didn't give the kid up easy." MacClough let go of the wheel and held up his right hand, fingers spread wide. "It took all five empties before he gave me the location."

"So before I could tell him he was under arrest and that he had the right to remain silent, he . . ." MacClough put his right index finger in his mouth and pulled a make-believe trigger. "He clamped his thumbs around my trigger finger and swallowed the bullet."

"Just like that?"

"Just like that, as God is my witness. Boom! He gave up the kid and offed himself. For more than twenty years, I wondered about that."

"You don't wonder anymore?" I asked.

"No, not anymore."

"Why not?"

He deflected my question. "You are one nosy Jewish son of a bitch. It doesn't matter why I don't wonder anymore. I just don't. I didn't want to go away before I told you about Hernandez."

"What about my brother?"

"Later for your brother." He parked in front of the Scupper. "I've got to check on something. C'mon in and let me buy ya a beer."

I thought about resisting, but I knew he'd drag me in by my ears if I put up too much of a stink. When MacClough wants to buy you a beer, you let him. It looked dark and pretty dead inside, sort of like I'd felt since Kira's murder. Yet, just the sight of the place, no matter how bereft of patrons, brightened my spirits. It lifted me up like the smell of a Nathans hot dog. Walking through the front door, I noticed the bar really was dark and empty. I shrugged my shoulders. For all I knew this could be one of MacClough's lame promotions: *Hide and go seek night! All lite beers half price if you can find them in the dark.*

"Surprise!" someone shouted.

The lights came up as did about twenty heads from

behind the bar. My brothers and sisters-in-law were there. Zak and the other kids, too. Guppy came out of the kitchen with Valencia Jones on his arm. Detective Fazio and Sergeant Hurley, looking fine in black jeans, boots, and work shirt, were seated at a booth. Sure I noticed Hurley. I was grieving, not dead myself. All of Sound Hill's usual suspects were on hand as well. Even Larry Feld had deigned to come and I was never happier to see the prick. But I was most shocked at the presence of my agent, Shelley Stickman.

"Dylan, Dylan, Dylan." He ran up to me smiling like he had a stale croissant stuck in his lips. "I got news."

"You got news, Shelley?" I was so enthusiastic I nearly fell back asleep.

"Sure I got news. What da ya think, this is a welcome back from the funeral party?"

"You're an asshole, Shelley."

"Sure I'm an asshole," he said straight-faced. "It's a prerequisite in my line of work."

"Get to the point, Shelley."

"Moviemax bought the rights. They're not crazy about the title, but for what they paid, they're allowed not to like the title. Sure," he winked, "the thing will probably never get made, but who cares?"

"You're right, Shelley," I said, shaking his hand unconsciously, "who cares?"

"Sure, bust my balls, but I got a heart. It's just not good for me to show the bastards I've got to deal with for you. I'm sorry about the girl."

"Thanks, Shelley."

"Ten percent is my thanks, but you're welcome anyway."

God, he was such a *putz*. Polonius was his role model. Maybe later we could get him to stand behind a curtain and the rest of us could play Hamlet. Doesn't everyone want to play Hamlet once in their career?

Valencia Jones walked up to me with tears in her eyes. Her mouth moved as if she wanted words to come out. None did. That was all right. She didn't have to say a word for me to understand. We hugged and I told her to give up skiing.

186

She liked that. I sat down with Hurley and Fazio. Hurley excused herself and asked me if she could bring me a drink on the way back. I explained that MacClough would know what I wanted. She drifted into the crowd. As she did, I thanked Fazio for saving our lives.

"Glad to do it." He smiled. "Almost like being a real cop."

"You know, MacClough didn't kill Hernandez," I said awkwardly.

"I know. He told me all about it."

"Why'd you help him? MacClough and my brother ruined your career."

"They didn't ruin it, they changed it. And I helped him, because he needed help. I don't hold what your brother might have done against you or your nephew. I'm an honorable man. Anyways, he helped me solve Caliparri's murder."

Confused, I wondered: "You're not bitter?"

"I didn't say that."

"What are you saying?"

He put his face close to mine. "Listen, MacClough came to me and asked for help. It wasn't complicated. I was just supposed to keep tabs on him when he went back to Riversborough. He figured he needed somebody to watch his flank. Thinking ahead, we arranged a meeting spot in case he got jammed up. If he needed it, I'd wire him for sound. IAD cops are good with wires. I hedged my bets and let the DEA in on our little arrangements. MacClough ran. We met. I wired him. We got the evidence. You got your nephew. All MacClough did for me was answer some questions, questions that have eaten my guts out for more than twenty years. Whether I liked the answers I got didn't really matter. It was that I got them. That's all. The past doesn't change. The hurt don't go away." He grabbed his belly. "The bitterness is still in me, but maybe I can sleep a little bit now."

Fazio stood up as Hurley returned with my drink. She was nursing a glass of champagne. She seemed ill at ease when she sat down.

"I know you're grieving, but . . ." She cleared her throat, hesitated, her face reddening. "This is awkward, but when

187

you're feeling better would it be all right with you if I took you to dinner sometime?"

I didn't answer right away.

"I know this is odd for you," she said, "but it's no good for me pretending that I don't like you. And don't be valiant or anything. Catching you on the rebound is better than not catching you at all."

Now I hesitated. "Listen. Sergeant—"

"—Cathy," she corrected.

"I don't know if I'm ready, Cathy."

"That's okay," she lied.

"Maybe some other time."

"Please, I'd like that."

As she excused herself, I found myself reaching for her hand.

"What is it?" she wondered.

"I think I changed my mind," I said. "Is that invitation for dinner still on the table?"

"Sure."

"Give me two weeks, okay?"

"Two weeks?" She winked. "I can wait two weeks."

I wrote my number down on a bar nap, stood and kissed her cheek. I spilled some of my Black and Tan on her shoes. I don't think she noticed.

"Two weeks," she reminded me.

"Better call or I'll come looking for you."

"I'd hate that," she purred.

Smiling with substance for the first time in weeks, I continued making the rounds. As I moved through the crowd, I received an odd mixture of congratulation and condolence. MacClough was in his element, pouring beers and weaving tales to anyone who would listen. They all listened. I knew his stories by heart as if they'd been passed onto me for safe-keeping, but I could listen to them still. He had the gift of making them fresh with each recounting. As I finished my pint, I lip-synced the words along with John as he captivated Guppy and my brother Josh with one of his favorites: the one about walking off his traffic post in Coney Island on the Fourth of July so he could bang a Puerto Rican nurse in the back of an ambulance. MacClough caught me watching, gave me a nod, and kept going without missing a beat.

Before John got to the part where his captain catches him with the nurse, Larry Feld grabbed me by the elbow and ushered me to a more private part of the room. Larry understood very little about people beyond greed and desperation. He had always been too hungry and ambitious himself to notice much else. But Larry understood pain. It was the engine of his life, though I doubt he ever thought of it as such. And for the first time since his mother's funeral, I saw real sorrow in his eyes. He held my hand as he held it that day. This time, however, it was his hand pulling *me* up from the depths. When he noticed the first hints of appreciation in my expression, he let go of my hand and disappeared.

*   *   *

The bulk of the crowd had turned into pumpkins and rats well before the witching hour. There were only a few of us left. MacClough, of course. Fazio and Hurley, like any two self-respecting cops, were in it until last call. Jeffrey, looking for his heart in a bottle of single malt scotch, was lingering in a corner somewhere. Bob Street from the Star Spangled Deli and old man Carney, the proprietor of Carney's Cabs, were playing a game of Buzz at the end of the bar with shots of Remy Martin and Grand Marnier. Card-carrying Bud drinkers, Street and Carney had expensive tastes when someone else was picking up the tab.

Curious, I wandered over to Jeffrey's lonely corner. "Did you pay for this?" I asked.

Staring oddly at the bottle, he seemed not to understand the question. Then, realizing I wasn't asking about the scotch, but the party, he had a good laugh at himself. It was a rare sight, seeing my big brother laugh at himself.

"I paid for part of it," he said. "Does it matter?"

"I guess not, not really." I sat down across from him. "I think there are some things we need to get out in the open."

"Cut to the chase, little brother."

"Was it your idea to cover-up what happened between MacClough and Hernandez?"

"It's not like you to be euphemistic, Dylan. What's this 'what happened between' crap?" Jeff pointed to the bar. "Your buddy over there blew a suspect's brains out and I turned him into a hero detective. So sue me."

"MacClough says it was suicide," I defended.

"Sure it was, little brother. Christ, I don't know. Maybe he's telling the truth. Maybe he's convinced himself that's what really happened. It's a rather moot point, don't you think?"

"So John made detective on the strength of a corpse and Fazio's career."

"Careers have turned on much less. MacClough was in the right place at the right time. It was his street contacts that led him to Hernandez, not mine. He was a damned beat cop, for chrissakes, a uniform. If he had just let it alone, worked his shifts and gone home, history would have been very different for all of us. But once he stuck his nose into things, he became the beneficiary of circumstance."

"Or," I differed, "its victim."

"Or its victim."

"But why the cover-up? Why not—"

"Because," Jeffrey cut me off, "police corruption was rampant then. The department was in disarray, still reeling from the Knapp Commission. There had even been some rumblings of state or federal intervention. The last thing the NYPD needed at that moment was the fallout from a rogue cop torturing and killing a suspect. Remember, cops were still called pigs back then. Hernandez would've been seen as a convenient minority fall guy, another victim of the big bad police. So I seized the moment. Me, the ambitious little pissant A.D.A., turned a sow's ear into a career for myself and a gold shield for your friend. With a bit of cooperation from the police brass—they were so fucking desperate to preserve their precious department, they would have done almost anything—MacClough's promise to keep his mouth shut and a few favors from the press, I spun a potential disaster into shining glory." Looking almost wistful, he said: "It's too bad, really, you couldn't have seen the headlines."

"Oh, but I did."

He didn't seem to hear what I said and, as he continued

to speak, Jeffrey gestured with his hands, framing imaginary headlines that floated somewhere above our table:

"HERO COP BEATS FEDS TO THE PUNCH"

I snapped my fingers in front of his face to break the trance.

"God, Dylan," he went on, "those were heady days. It was perfect. All the rumblings from Albany and Washington came to an abrupt halt. So if you are asking me whether the life of one scumbag kidnapper and the career of one honest cop was worth it, I'd say it was. If Fazio knew all the details, *he'd* agree."

"Okay, Jeff, I just wanted to hear it from your own lips."

Standing now, he said: "I haven't properly thanked you for getting Zak back to us."

"Forget it. His being safe should be enough thanks for both of us."

"When did you get so smart?" he teased.

"Obviously, when you weren't looking."

"Save my seat. I want you to tell me about Kira." He brushed his hand gently across my cheek. "I may never have met her, but I know she was too good for you."

Jeffrey could not have known how much the world would change before he got back to his seat.

Bob Street and old man Carney had had enough. They held each other, zig zagging their way to the Scupper's door. Once at the threshold, however, they were at a bit of a loss. I set them free, pushing open the door. The two of them stumbled onto the pavement, laughing. I watched them stagger on down the otherwise silent street until they disappeared fully into the night. The cool salty air felt good on my face and made a home for itself in my lungs, but I could feel exhaustion tapping at my shoulder. I looked forward to a lengthy visit with my bed. In some sense I was relieved that Kira and I had never shared that bed. If we had, I could never have slept there again.

As I began to pull the door shut, I could still hear Bob Street and Carney laughing like giddy poltergeists moving onto their next haunt. I never did get the door closed. Another hand, a powerful hand held it open. I could say little about the man on the opposite side of the door other than he had a steel grip and was bathed in darkness. Beyond that, he was a mystery.

"Sorry," I said, "private party."

"I'm looking for MacClough, man," was his answer to that. "I think he's expecting me."

The muscles in my arm ached from holding the door against his grip. I called to MacClough, still *futzing* around behind the bar, and told him there had been a request for an audience.

"If I'm expectin' the man, let him in."

And in that instant I let go of the door, I knew something was wrong. The night visitor yanked the door open and came charging into the bar out of his darkness. He was a short, well-muscled latino dressed in fatigue pants and a white tank top. His exposed skin was a maze of grotesque tattoos, the tank top preventing me from making sense of the stains on his body. He sported a pinstripe-thin moustache above a wicked gray goatee. His scalp was shaved and his eyes were black and feral. They saw nothing but their prey, Johnny MacClough.

"Hey *pato*," he hissed at MacClough, "you know who I am?"

"I've been waitin' for you, Angel."

Wild eyes almost smiled at that. "So you got my letter."

Fazio, passive until now, jumped to his feet when he heard Angel's name. He reached for his ankle. Hurley too went for her gun. Suddenly, Angel saw more than MacClough.

"This is for my brother," Angel screamed, spitting, his hand disappearmg behind his back. When his hand reappeared, it held a sawed-off shotgun.

I jumped at him, but he flicked me away like ashes. I followed the barrel of the gun to MacClough's eyes. They held no fear that I could see. Maybe I was invested in not seeing any. His eyes were impatient. Come on, they seemed to say, let's get it over with. I remember yelling at Fazio and Hurley to do something. And then Jeffrey threw open the mens room door. It was human to look, to hesitate just a beat. But Angel was not human. The little shotgun coughed thunder, spit smoke and fire. The impact caught John squarely, freeing him from the restrictions of gravity. The beveled mirror on the bar's back wall ended his brief flight. John slid to the floor, a shower of shattered glass and spirits anointing his body.

Fazio and Hurley cut Angel to pieces almost before the scatter shot hit MacClough. As far as doing Johnny any good, it could have been a month later. The damage was done. Angel sprawled out, his head landing with a crack at my feet. The bullet holes had rendered his tattoos forever nonsensical.

John was lifeless behind the bar. There would be no good-byes. The four of us, Fazio and Hurley, Jeffrey and myself, formed a circle around his body. Glass crunched under our feet. More out of reflex than hope, Fazio knelt down and touched his fingers to Johnny's bloodied throat. There was nothing to feel but the heat running out of him.

"I'll go make the call," Hurley volunteered.

Then Fazio said something only survivors say: "It's better this way."

He must have seen the confusion in my eyes and answered my question before I asked it.

"Liver cancer," he said, "and it was spreading. He wanted to tell you, but with your dad, the kid, and the girl, he just never had the heart."

I guess Fazio was right. It was better this way. John was haunted by his own father's death from cancer.

Pointing at Angel, Jeffrey asked: "Who was he?"

"Angel Hernandez," Fazio answered.

"Hernandez!" The name caught in my throat.

"That's right, Klein, the kidnapper's brother," Fazio confirmed. "MacClough told me Angel had sworn to get even for his little brother."

Sirens replaced the laughter of giddy poltergeists as the soundtrack for the evening. Tires screeched. The Scupper was crowded once again. John always liked it when the Scupper was crowded.

We passed the school where children played
Their lessons scarcely done;
We passed the fields of gazing grain,
We passed the setting sun.

—Emily Dickinson

Epilogue

Different Shades

I had met many of John's friends in the time we'd known one another. But I never realized what a small percentage that was until the funeral. In a way it was a shame that I met some of the faces I had only known through John's stories. The reality could never match the broad brush of his words.

The funeral was held at St. Mark's, MacClough's old Brooklyn church and parochial school. A member of the Emerald Society played the bagpipes from the balcony and one of his old schoolyard chums sang "Danny Boy." Even the priest could not hide his tears. Half of Sound Hill was there, even some of the upper-crust summer vacationers took the time to say their good-byes. I had no idea where Angel Hernandez was buried.

Walking my share of his coffin down the center aisle of the church, my arm ached as if it was carrying three bodies. My father's death, Kira's, and now Johnny's were pulling me down. Too much of my universe had disappeared all at once. I thought my arm would float up after we slid John's coffin into the hearse.

Outside the church, there was the usual confusion about who was riding in what car and with whom. I had to bum a ride for Shelley Stickman, who was so worried about where I was going to find a new technical adviser that he had neglected to make his own arrangements. I grabbed Larry Feld and asked that he ride with me. Larry seemed surprised by the invitation, but didn't put up a fight. I pointed him to the car and told him to wait for me there.

I found Detective Fazio lighting up a Kent at the side of the church steps. We shook hands. He said all the things people say. He offered me a cigarette. I took one.

"I hear MacClough left you the bar," Fazio said, holding his lighter to the tip of my cigarette.

"Me and his brother." I handed him an envelope. "Here. I found this in MacClough's papers. It's addressed to you. Open it up."

"I don't have to."

And before I could ask why not, he held his lighter to the

corner of the envelope. He held it between his fingers until it was fully ablaze and then dropped it to the sidewalk. We watched the ball of ashes evaporate in the wind.

Checking the tips of his fingers for burns, Fazio said: "I guess you're curious."

"Always."

"It was MacClough's sworn affidavit about the kidnapping and the coverup. MacClough promised it to me when he came to me for help."

"Why'd you destroy it?" I was puzzled. "You could have used it to prove you were right back then, that you were the victim of a cover-up. You could have sued the city, the department."

"Statute of limitations," he said.

"Since when are you a lawyer?"

"Not the state's limitations. My own."

Car horns cried out as Cathy Hurley found us.

"There you two are. Everybody's waiting for you, Dylan."

"I'm coming." I smiled at her and turned to go.

"Hey, Klein," Fazio called to me. "If you need a barman, let me know. I'm pretty good with a beer pull."

"What about the Castle-on-Hudson PD?" I wondered.

"No more make-believe for me," he said. "Being around MacClough reminded me what it was like to be around real cops."

"He would have appreciated that. Thanks."

I led the procession in John's fully restored '66 Thunderbird. I guess in his way John was trying to let me know he was dying. But when you assume a man will live forever, you don't notice even the most obvious hints. Or maybe my father's long crawl to death had blinded me. It was just another thing I would never know.

Rather than heading directly to the cemetery, I circled the block so that MacClough could pass the basketball courts behind the church one final time. Some kids were playing half-court and couldn't be bothered to stop to contemplate mortality. Although I did not know him then, I could picture John as a kid, not stopping to look. He wouldn't've seen the value in it. Everybody was going to die someday.

Larry Feld just sat quietly, taking it all in. St. Mark's was, after all, on the border of our old neighborhood. He frowned as we passed back in front of the church. I don't suppose Larry ever understood my affection for anyone who wasn't Jewish. As a child raised to believe in a world that consisted only of victims and victimizers, Larry had a clear sense of which role Jews historically played. Sure, most of his clients were gentiles, but that just felt like payback to Larry. It gave him a sense of superiority, power. I think Larry saw my friendships and dealings with non Jews as vaguely treasonous. The truth was that Larry saw my affection for anyone else as tantamount to betrayal.

"It's freezing in here," Larry moaned as we sped down the Belt Parkway with the T-Bird's windows wide open.

"Is it?"

"So, why'd you ask me to ride with you?"

"I wanted to thank you for your help," I said.

"Frankly, Dylan, I would have preferred a nice bottle of Laurent-Perrier 1991. Riding in the lead car of a funeral procession for a guy I didn't particularly care for isn't my idea of thanks."

"It's the best I could do on short notice. Besides," I admitted, "I wanted to talk to you."

"About what, your murderous friend back there in the hearse?"

"It was suicide," I shouted.

"Murder comes in different shades, Dylan. If you wanna call it suicide, go right ahead. There's no one left to argue the point."

"Okay, Larry, let's drop it. I just wanted you to ride with me."

"Why?"

"Because, for all your goddamn faults, you're my oldest friend."

I caught him smiling out of the corner of my eye.

"I have faults?" he said.

The car was silent again but for the sound of the wind. Larry didn't even complain about the cold. Despite his protestations to the contrary, it meant a lot to Larry that I'd asked him to ride with me. I knew John would have approved. Friendship meant everything to Johnny MacClough.

In the rearview mirror I watched the long line of head-lights snake into the cemetery. Now John might finally rest in peace. I didn't know that I was likely to, not for a while, anyway.